Bad Elf

JOHN RAE

ISBN: 0692963138
ISBN-13: 978-0692963135

For Emma.

1 - CHRISTMAS CANCELLED!

Holy hell, it's cold!

That's about all Jackie Rumpus might have to say about life at The Pole, except that it is also dark and dreary. And muted. And desolate—with a bitter and biting swirling wind. You won't find it on any map, but The Pole is a snowy campus nestled in the valley between seven mountains known collectively as The Crown. The path into this world tucks between a gap between the Crown's tines...where legend says a mountain once stood, but was stolen. Can you believe that? A mountain...stolen? Even if you could steal a mountain, what good would stealing one do?

Anywho...The Pole, of course, has more to it than cold and mountains. The campus itself mixes new buildings and old, fantastic cottages. And, of course, it also has reindeer—housed in a small, red and weathered barn way off campus because, let's face it, reindeer stink. And in such a place where *downwind* happens to be in just about every direction, it is best to keep the beasts away.

And, of course, The Pole has Santa Claus, whose familiar black boots crunched through the snow to the

1

reindeer barn to spend a few minutes of his day with his oldest friends—Dasher, Dancer, Prancer, Vixen, Comet, Cupid, Donner, and Blitzen. Oh! And Rudolf. We can't forget Rudy. Santa's team. They had been with Santa on many Christmas Eve adventures, and even more less-Christmasy adventures. Often, it took just a few moments, checking in with them to calm Santa from an otherwise crabby day. Today was one of those crabby days. Come to think of it, most days lately have been crabby days, with Santa holed up in his corner office at North Pole Headquarters, fumbling over a problem he couldn't quite place. Something troubled him, but Santa couldn't figure out what. And unfortunately for Santa, today's visit with his team would offer no relief from said crabbiness…it would make it only worse. But it just might help expose what was troubling him.

He reached the small barn, creaked open the doors, and flipped a set of those old-timey knife switches—the kind that spark and smell of ozone when thrown—and a series of lights flickered brighter, illuminating row after row of reindeer pens, several stories high. Now, you might wonder how so many reindeer could fit inside such a tiny, old barn, but things at The Pole aren't always what they seem. For in addition to cold, and reindeer, and Santa, The Pole had magic. Polar Magic.

"Boys and girls!" Santa called. The reindeer met his greeting with braying and lowing, grunting. The pens closest to the doors held his team, and each was marked with an ancient and weathered wooden nameplate, written in the long, scrolling lettering the elves fancied. As Santa stepped over to the pen with Blitzen's nameplate, he tripped on a small, tan, saddle that some rogue elf had forgotten to put away. "Son of a-" he winced, catching his words before tumbling down with a strained "ho...ho...ho."

A concerned red glow brightened from Rudolf's pen. Santa's leg had bent at just the wrong place! Bent at just the wrong angle! Not merely sprained or strained, but clearly broke. And so very close to Christmas Eve.

Several minutes later, he hobbled into the bright-white infirmary...the Elf Hospital tucked neatly in the corner of Headquarters. With every step, he winced and grumped, leaning on a shovel that smelled like the parting end of a reindeer. The Elf Nurse took his shovel and led Santa past the large center fireplace, past rows of mostly-empty elf-sized beds to one of the two grown-human-sized beds that rarely ever saw use. Now, you might be wondering on the size of an elf-sized bed. Well, most elves would come up to just over Santa's knee, and the Elf Nurse was no different. She grunted under the weight of Santa's hobbling, for he leaned his entire weight onto her cap—a regular flip-front nurse cap, but whose top draped down the back in a long, candy-striped stocking. Her bright-white uniform refused to let go of a few cherry-colored stains from patients suffering from the Sugarplum Trinkles over the years. "Oof!" she grunted, the bell on the end of her cap rattling with each step until The Missus rushed in and took her husband's weight.

"It's broke," Santa grumbled towards the bed. "Tripped over a saddle." His frustration sneaked away from him in the way he enunciated *saddle*, baring his teeth.

The Missus sat next to him on the bed and let the Elf Nurse inspect the leg. "I tell ya, if you're going to go joy-riding you should bring someone to help." She rubbed his back. "For moments like this!"

"I wasn't riding. Just visiting. It was one of the elves. Left the saddle on the floor. Probably left in a hurry because they were riding one of my team." The Elf Nurse and The Missus gasped. "I know, right? How many times do I warn them that nobody rides Santa's team except Santa?" He grunted, but then howled in pain as sparks fizzled from the Elf Nurse's hands over his leg.

"Well, that will set it," she said. "But I still need to put it in a cast."

"Snowballs," Santa grumbled, folding his arms across his chest.

The Missus watched him pout. "What can you do?" she finally asked. "Can't just cancel Christmas."

Santa turned an eye on her…now there was an idea. "I'm so annoyed right now. I don't feel very Christmasy."

"Nonsense, dear. You haven't been very Christmasy all year." On his sharp glance, she added, "Just saying. If we followed the Chinese calendar, this would be the Year of The Crab. Not that they traditionally have Crab Years, mind you."

"You're not very comforting."

"You've been so crabby, I think your butt just might be forming an exoskeleton," she smiled with a wink. It was a subtle smile, and an equally subtle wink, but they had the most not-so-subtle effect on melting Santa's heart. She always made him smile. And once he did so, she leaned into him for a hug as the Elf Nurse wrapped his leg. "I'm sorry you broke your leg. And I'm sorry for whatever it is that's been troubling you. I wish you would talk to me about it."

"I wish I knew what *it* was." And this was no lie, for the amount of time he spent trying to figure it out had grown from hours to days, weeks and months. He'd sit at his desk, staring at his computer screen, sometimes crushing candy, sometimes distracting himself with social media and finding whose Instapic snapshots might warrant an entry on the Naughty List. And though it looked like might just be goofing off, he was always wondering what to do about *something*.

But what was that thing?

"Do you know who's been riding your team?"

"I've my suspicions. The question is…" He trailed off, nodding his forefinger against his nose. "What to do about it?"

By all accounts, the factory floor of the Toy Shoppe was a happy sweatshop—bright, colorful, warm— where row after row of festive elves worked tirelessly at their workstations, making toys, singing along to holiday music. They moved at a feverish pace, to you and me, zipping along with their hand tools and such…but to them their pace seemed pretty normal.

But then there was Jack, who hardly moved at all. As a matter of fact, if Jack could not move at all, he'd be not moving at a feverish elf-pace. But, of course, he couldn't not move *at all*, certainly not with the angry music blasting in his earbuds. He sat on his work stool, bopping along and tapping a candy-striped ring against the table top of his workstation. In his early twenties, Jack had reached the point in his life where even though he wasn't quite an adult, he was expected to be, well, more adult-like. Like Santa, he felt stuck. But, unlike Santa, Jack knew what his problem was, and he knew what he needed to do. He needed a change. As he tapped that ring to the music, he fantasized about what he planned to do.

His eyes, circled by dark eyeliner, stared off into space under a curly mop of jet-black-dyed hair. He wore a pale make-up to hide the natural rosiness of his cheeks, but he looked as dark and cold as the outside. The fake piercings and intentionally-torn clothes were Jack's way of saying, "If you're going to look at me, don't look at *me*." Folks at The Pole didn't know what to make of him. He was restless, bored, angry, a loner, weird, and well, very un-elf-like.

Even the things that made him happy and excitable were odd. Most all the elves, for example, idolized Santa. But not Jack. He idolized Krampus. Like some rock-star roadie, across the back of his red work vest, Jack had dramatically etched his idol's name. And who is Krampus? A demon. A Christmas demon. A demon whose job is to punish the naughtiest of children on Christmas Eve.

But there was something else that made Jack happy and excitable…Candi Kane. Candi was more like your stereotypical, bright-eyed, elf. A stark contrast to Jack, the only hint of darkness in her was her necklace pendent—a jack o' lantern bat, made festive with a Santa hat. "Jackie!" she shouted, yanking out his earbuds and startling him from his daydream.

"Gah! What?" He quickly put the candy-striped ring on his middle finger.

"Don't you want to win the contest?" She pointed to the factory wall, to a large poster that showed a happy elf riding alongside Santa on a snowy night, delivering presents. It read:

RIDE WITH SANTA!

Jack turned to his small stack of half-baked, pathetic toys. A few were truly inspired, but with Jack's own dark twist. His latest doll, for example, was of a bride. A corpse-bride. Emptiness peered out from her button eyes; empty, yet thoughtful; as if her mind twisted upon itself every bit as much as the horns that spiraled out from her head. Jack picked her up and admired that dark gaze. "Nope," he said, as if the answer to Candi's question should be obvious. Why *would* he want to ride with Santa?

Santa charged into the factory on the catwalk overlooking the elves. He hobbled on his cane, sporting a leg cast. Here, in front of the elves, it was easier to see he was not the jolly, fat elf we expect. Instead, he was more of a grumpy dad. Towering over the elves, he grunted in disgust, throwing down the saddle over which he had tripped. Work stopped as everyone gave him their curious attention. Eying Jack, Santa grumbled, "Someone has been sneaking Rudolf out for a joyride! How many times do I have to tell you that nobody flies Santa's team, but Santa?" A collective gasp from the elves nearly sucked the air from the room. Candi turned to Jack, wide-eyed. Jack mouthed that it wasn't him. "The Missus says, and The Missus is right…Christmas is cancelled!"

Heartbroken, the elves all mumbled and groaned, turning to one another…surprised and confused. But nobody was more upset than Jack. He kicked at the table leg and marched straight up to Santa, bounding up the stacked presents on up to the catwalk, coming nearly face-to-kneecap. The rosiness of his cheeks burned, shining through the make-up. "Rumplemints!" He stomped his foot. "You can't just *cancel* Christmas!"

"Language, Rumpus." Santa shot Jack a very dad-like warning glare. But it was more than just a dad-like warning glare. Once the frown gave way to an arched right eyebrow, and a sigh escaped Santa's lips, and his head cocked just slightly askew, and his left cheek pulled in a slight twist, the warning glare had finished morphing into what the elves called *The Santa Look*. And it was an annoyed, somewhat pained, look that was used almost exclusively for Jack.

Jack breathed heavily as they stared down one another, until finally Jack broke. "Christmas ain't yours to cancel." Everyone turned on Jack…un-be-lievable. And the leers and jeers didn't end as their shift suddenly ended and the elves all made their way back to their dorms. All through the crowded hall, elves bumped him, nudged him, poked him and did what he hated most…they looked at him, with glaring eyes, of course, all giving him grief for getting Christmas cancelled. Candi did her best to chase after him.

"Way to go, Snowflake!" Feliz snapped, just as he pushed Jack up against the wall and held him there.

What Feliz lacked in height, he made up for in stockiness…unusual in both, in regards to an elf.

Feliz's taller-and-skinnier-than-usual crony, Mickie, chimed in. "I busted my jingle bells trying to win that contest!" Mickie's elf hat flipped forward from him snapping his neck so hard with anger.

Jack remained calm. "I didn't cancel Christmas."

Candi tugged to get Feliz's arm off Jack. "Why do you hang around this loser?" he snapped at her. And when he bumped her away, that is when Jack lost his cool. Jack grunted, kicked forward and slammed Feliz against the opposite wall.

"You gotta problem with me? Fine!" he snarled. "You don't touch Candi."

And now Candi tugged at Jack's arm, flustered in trying to calm everyone down. "It's all right, Jackie!"

"It's Jack!" he shouted, before releasing Feliz.

Feliz adjusted the collar on his workshop vest, watching Jack walk away before finally hissing just loud enough, "Freak!"

"Feliz…" Jack stopped, stomped back to Feliz. "We live at The Pole. We dress like this. Make toys so that some jolly guy can deliver them on to people who put weirdly-decorated trees in their living rooms. Trees, in their living rooms!" Jack shook his head. "You ever think we might all be freaks?" He stared into Feliz's empty expression for a moment before storming away.

Candi paused in his wake, sighing, before catching up to Jack. "I don't understand you, Jackie. Why do you hate Santa so much?"

"I don't hate him," he shrugged, pushing through the crowd.

Jack reached his room. The nameplate on his door had been marked up so that JACKIE RUMPUS now read JACK KRUMPUS. His own Goth scribbles flourished across his door—flying skulls, lurking ghosts, strange fantastical creatures that came from his own imagination—like a patched, stitched-up, rag-doll puppy with deep, hollow, eyes and a flaming tail—and, of course, a doodle of his idol, Krampus. In addition to those doodles, vandals had marked his door with very un-Christmasy words and images. *Freak*, *Loser*, and *Snowflake* peppered depictions such as Jack getting run over by a reindeer. Jack never bothered to remove the vandalism, for he found the irony of their hate juxtaposed with anti-Christmas sentiments slightly homey. Nobody ever understood his joke.

Candi caught up to him again. "Then why do you act like you hate Santa? Or care if Christmas is cancelled?"

Jack twisted with a pointed finger. "Every year we get a single Christmas wish. Just one!" As he turned back to fuss with the lock, "I have the same wish every year. To meet Krampus. And fat man never comes through. Never." He looked Candi in the eye to make his point. "Santa. Hates. Me." He opened the door to illuminate the dark room, exposing more darkness, even after he turned on the lights. Posters of Goth bands wallpapered the tiny room, along with vintage-looking posters for Krampus. *Greetings from the Krampus*, read one poster—

showing a horned devil with rather playful eyes. *The Christmas Demon*, read another—showing a shadow of a tall horned figure with one human leg and one goat leg, hauling a basket full of children over his shoulder. Antoher *The Devil of Christmas* showed a horned Krampus behaving rather naughty with a scantily-clad woman. *Krampusnacht* showed him as white and furry, different from the others that showed him black and hairy. And finally, Jack's favorite poster showed a threatening Krampus, towering over frightened and cowering children. Very prominently, it read:

You've Been Naughty!

Candi looked about his otherwise oddly empty room with some suspicion and then back to the Krampus posters. "How can Santa deliver something that isn't real?"

"Krampus is *so* real."

"A story moms and dads use to trick kids into behaving for Christmas."

Jack raised an eyebrow. "Like Santa Claus?"

"Except Santa is real."

Jack slumped into a chair and pouted. "Why can't I just have something to believe in?"

Candi teased with a little sing-song jab. "You better not pout."

Jack glared up to her...not in the mood. He took off his ridiculous elf shoes. The tiny bell on the end of each was made up with devil horns, which not only paid homage to Jack's idol, but also muted their twinkling

11

and jingling into a dull thud. "I need Christmas uncancelled."

"I don't understand you, Jackie." She watched him stretch his toes in his striped stockings and felt a huge distance between the two of them. "We used to be best friends."

Jack frowned, looked up to her, confused. "We're friends." How could Candi feel otherwise? She was his only friend at The Pole, let alone *best* friend.

Candi looked about all the posters. "We're in different worlds."

"Right!" Jack sat up. "I don't belong here, Candi. You're the only one who can't see it. I hate The Pole. I hate making toys. I hate red. And green. And I hate our stupid elf names. And-"

"You hate my name?"

Jack rattled off names as if counting them on his fingers. "Jackie Rumpus. Candi Kane. Feliz Navidad. Mickie Rooney. Holly Pumpernickel." He shook his head. "And everyone thinks I'm nuts because I want to be just Jack."

Up with the air quotes. "Jack '*Krumpus*.'"

"So?"

Feeling like the distance might be just too great for her to handle in that moment, Candi turned to leave...and tripped over the opening for a Santa sack that stuck out from under the bed. Jack spun in his seat, their eyes locking for a moment as a secret just revealed itself. She snatched up the sack and dumped its contents onto the floor—and the room was suddenly un-oddly empty. Goth knickknacks, elf hats, his first wooden toy-making mallet, Jack's favorite pillow, his first toy robot, a picture of him and Candi as children—enjoying a laugh at Hollyberry Farms under the Northern Lights—a seemingly endless pile of Jack's belongings spilled out— more so than could possibly fit inside the bag. Yet, even so, after Candi gave the bag one final shake, and a tiny pair of underpants tumbled out, the sack still appeared to be filled with toys. She stood a moment, eyes angry and fixed on Jack, before throwing the sack at him. When it hit him, it collapsed flat. "Going somewhere, Jackie?"

Jack stared at the truck heap, thinking, before finally confessing, "I'm running away from The Pole. Christmas Eve. While he's away delivering presents."

Candi rolled her eyes, hurt that he wouldn't share this with her. Intentionally at least. "Where would you even go?"

"I'm gonna go live with Krampus."

She shook her head...you're nuts. "He's not real."

"He is," Jack insisted. "And I think, maybe-" He trailed off to find the right words. Something that would help her understand. "Maybe I just *belong* on a darker side of Christmas."

Her frustration escalated with each word. "He's. Not. Real!" She took in another look at the posters of his idol. "And even if he were, Jackie, he's evil."

"He's not evil!" Jack shot to his feet. "He just doesn't waste any time on the good kids. Only worries about the bad." Candi glared, unconvinced. "He and Santa used to even ride together! But now Santa does both jobs, and just gives bad kids a lump of coal. Whoop-de-do. And most of the time, he doesn't even bother doing that much." He thought a moment. "He's a little too stingy with the coal, if you ask me."

As if saying as much would show him the absurdity of what he believed, Candi sighed. "Meanwhile, Krampus drags them to Hell in a hand basket."

But this only got Jack excited. "I know, right?!"

Candi huffed, shook her head, feeling lost and overwhelmed in that distance between them. Like the Santa sack, that small space between them felt full of extra space, stuffed with something that seemed unnecessary and yet desperately needed. But all Candi could do in the moment was to let that distance (and Jack) just be.

2 - UN. CAN. CEL.

The reason you won't find The Pole—or The Crown, for that matter—on any map, is that it is protected by Polar Magic. As if encased in a giant snow globe, an invisible border lightly shimmers with the Northern Lights if someone who doesn't belong attempts to trek inside. Imagine you and a friend attempted the frigid journey north and made it to the border. Another step from you would send you clear to the other side of The Crown, and you wouldn't know what had happened. If you were then to turn back to your friend, you might be able to discern them in the very far distance, provided the weather was bright and sunshiny, which is rarely ever the case at The Pole. And in the distance between you and your friend, you wouldn't see The Pole, nor would you see the seven tines of The Crown. You'd just see the gap between you, and think one of you had gotten lost in the snow. But you certainly wouldn't ever know that Santa was near, for at The Pole there are only two types of people...those who belong there, and those who are invited.

And this fact was a huge deal for Jack, for he never knew to which group he belonged.

There are many types of magical creatures and several types of elves in the world. The Woodland Elves, for example, are stewards of forests and keepers of the dark. And, yes, the darkness must be kept. Zephyr Elves live in the clouds, and are more popularly known as Faeries…but don't ever call them that to their face. Never, ever, ever. The term is considered no so- politically correct. Zephyrs bring messages and battle with storms. Tinchers, often considered evil, are actually no more or less evil than Zephyrs, but they move through fire and their rage can be difficult to manage. The Toy Elves at The Pole are more properly known as Phantagrasons. They build things, are problem solvers, and they move really, really fast—zipping about in what seems like a normal fashion for them. Their creative drive makes them perfect for making toys, however, Phantagrasons lack direction. Tell a typical toy elf to make a stuffed animal, for example, and their most creative spark turns into a child's amusement. But don't tell a Phantagrason to make a stuffed animal, and the elf may sit idly—frustrated perhaps because they feel like they should be doing something, but unsure what it is they should be doing. And that is where Santa comes in. He directs them, plans for them, takes care of them, and gives them focus that every day should be the next Christmas Eve and their reward of happy children all the world over…for a happy child most definitely is their kind of magic.

And Jack…he had drive. And this set him apart from all the other elves; further apart than his make-up and clothes and such had already set him apart. He didn't particularly like all the things that Phantagrasons liked. And he rarely seemed happy. But there was something else that set Jack apart from the others, and it was actually something he had in common with them.

Nobody really knew if Jack belonged at The Pole, or if he had been invited.

Elves aren't magically hatched into the world...they have parents just the same as you and I, but Jack was also an orphan. Those in the know didn't really know much of anything other than one day a baby Jack just showed up. And the question was...did he belong there, or was he invited? Santa hadn't much to say about the situation other than to tell folks to mind their own business. That, of course, Jack belonged there. The Pole was his home.

But Jack never did like what the other elves liked. And he was too tall to be a Faerie, yet figurative storms brooded about him. The darkness suggested Woodland...but Jack was a million times too short to be a Woodland Elf. The passion and rage suggested maybe Tincher...if you were to squint just right. He seemed to be a toy elf, but he also seemed to be something else, too. Only Santa knew for sure, and Santa wasn't talking...not even to Jack, who had asked the question once or twice. Santa would always reiterate that The Pole was his home, knowing that that wasn't really what Jack was asking. So still, Jack's question loomed...did he belong there, or was he invited?

On a normal day, Jack took a bit of time getting ready. After all, it took effort to put on his make-up, and add the trinkets to his eyes, nose, and ears, and have his clothes torn just right to create the illusion of not caring. But today was not normal. He didn't have to work in the Toy Shoppe, and he needed to create the illusion of caring.

Gone was the make-up that made his face pale. Gone was the eye-liner that made his eyes serious. Gone were the trinkets that made it so his face looked full of holes. Gone were the torn clothes. Rather than putting on regular every day elf clothes, however, Jack put on his best outfit—a black suit and tie he hadn't worn since some ancient funeral. The mirror reflected a proper elf, and as Jack mustered up courage to do what he had to do, he kept finding reasons to procrastinate. Like the black mop atop his head. Unruly. Very Rumpus-like. He combed it down, re-wetting it and re-gelling it, over and over and over again, but he could not get it to look serious enough. It seemed as if he might be able to get it just right, only to have a hair or two out of place, but by the time he fought those hairs into place, the mop had returned.

"Crumpets!"

A knock on the door was welcomed relief. It was Candi, who was already in the middle of a sentence by the time he opened the door and she had got a good look at him. "Well," she paused, with a smile. "Look at you!"

Jack's eyebrows arched up. "What's wrong with me?"

"Nothing," she said, adjusting his tie. "Did someone die?"

He shook his head. "I have to go and see Santa. Gotta get Christmas uncancelled."

Candi frowned. Her hand dropped from his tie. "So you can run away?" Jack nodded. "I was going to see if you wanted to get breakfast, but you got plans." She turned away.

"Maybe afterwards?" he jumped. "I can come get you."

Candi turned back to Jack's smile. And his smile made her smile. She caressed his bare cheek with the back of her hand, causing Jack's face to twist up in question. "It's been a long while since I've seen you without all that crap on."

"I like that crap."

"I know you do. I had forgotten how soft your eyes could look." Her gaze hovered on his for a moment before she turned away. "Breakfast when you're done." Her long, blonde bob swayed as she sprited away.

Bright-eyed and curious, Jack walked through the wide office space of North Pole Headquarters, making his way to a large corner office where the nameplate read S. CLAUS. He paused for courage, looking about the cube farm and wondering what it would be like to work there instead of at the Toy Shoppe. He knocked at the door. No answer. Knocked again and waited. And when it was clear that nobody was inside, he opened the door using a second, much lower doorknob placed just for the elves, and peered in.

Jack had already snuck inside before giving any thought to whether it was naughty or nice to simply let himself in. The obnoxiously long office struck him with awe. More corporate than festive, yet definitely Santa's personal space. As he snuck about, Jack gawked at everything—twenty-foot high bookshelves crammed with every Christmas story ever written, along with a few non-Christmas books from Santa's favorite authors. "Old Man and the Sea," he read, running his fingers along the book spines, and wondering just who was Earnest Hemmingway, or Mark Twain. He pulled out a book by a Stephen King. "Ooh! This looks like fun," he said, reading the back cover. "And…really, really scary," he added, putting the book back as if the demons it contained might spill out and into the chill he felt shimmering down his spine.

A large telescope, oddly fixed on Gumdrop Mountain, took center stage on the wide bay windows that overlooked the campus. Strange trinkets scattered about, as well as many, many Santa hats—and not just the style we're familiar with with the fuzzy white brim and poof ball. A formal red top hat, trimmed with hollyberry, rested atop a coat rack. Santa's favorite whimsical ones—like the ones that looked like a reindeer, or made with a silly spring—usually given to him as gifts from children—lined one of the walls with colorful, pointed Christmas hats and droopy red hoods, and old ornately decorated religious caps. Strangest of all, was an ancient, pale green and red elf hat with brushed nickel bells, resting by itself on a small stand near Santa's desk.

"Right!" Jack exclaimed, reminded that he was on a mission, but as he hurried his steps towards the desk, something else caught his attention, stopping him yet again—a large snow globe, bigger than Jack, and filled with a swirling ephemeral fog. He ran his fingers over the glass, and the swirls glowed and bended to his touch. Something hid inside the mist, and Jack tried to bend the swirls out of his way so he could see whatever it was, but he decided to give up the hunt as it continued to elude him.

bent

Jack turned towards Santa's desk and climbed into the large office chair. He was ridiculously small in the seat, but his beaming smile made up for lack of size. He pushed against the desk, trying to spin the chair, until something caught his eye. How his eyes grew!

"The Naughty List!" A post-it attached to the scroll read *Check this twice. Love, The Missus.*

"Rumpus!" Santa bellowed from the door. Jack yelped, jumped up and in his surprise, yanked the Naughty List and other bric-a-brac from the desktop into a scattering heap at his feet. When the papers all settled he peered from behind the desk to find that Santa had already zipped all the way to the desk, and was crouched down and peering right back at Jack. "What are you doing in my office?"

"Looking for you, sir," Jack tried in his most sincere sounding tone that didn't fool Santa a bit.

"Sir?" Santa huffed, unimpressed.

"You can't cancel Christmas."

"Because it is not mine to cancel, I presume?" Santa's eyebrows raised in a question…are we having this conversation again?

"I-I'm sorry about that," Jack flustered. "I was angry. Shocked! Christmas cancelled?"

Santa was slightly amused at the air quotes Jack had put up around the word *cancelled*. He towered up tall, tapping his cane against his cast. "Look at me, Jackie. My leg is broken." Jack tried his doe-y-est doe eyes and suggested that he could deliver presents for Santa. "Right," Santa chuckled. "Jackie Rumpus as Santa. Plan

B." Santa's deep hee-hee-hee's gradually morphed into an hysterical ho-ho-ho, driving a hurt Jack from the office.

But as Jack shut the door behind him, he realized it wasn't hurt he felt, for he never really expected Santa to warm up to the idea of Jack delivering presents Christmas Eve. Still, the ho-ho-ho's from the other side of the door zinged a little bit. "Plan B?" he thought. No, it wasn't hurt he felt at all. He felt *challenged*.

At breakfast, his new—but definitely going to be short-lived—look caught everyone's attention. And as he and Candi made their way through the food lines to the tables, the elves all did what Jack hated most…they looked at him. How he wished he had gone back to his room to put his costume on first.

"Who died?" asked Feliz, attempting to trip Jack. But even though Jack couldn't see Feliz's foot while carrying his tray of food, Jack had enough experience to know he needed to take an off-step to avoid tumbling. He tried to conjure a witty comeback, but his insecurities muddled his wit bit, and so he decided that ignoring Feliz might instead be the best decision. He and Candi sat down to breakfast where he gave her all the details about how things went not-so-well with Santa.

"I need a Plan B," he finally said.

"What's Plan B?"

Jack shrugged. "Gotta figure that out yet." Just then, Jack was hit in the face with cold serving of grits. The white, buttery corn meal dripped from his face. He wiped it from his eyes and was met with laughter from Feliz and Mickie.

"Not funny, Rooney!" Candi snapped, and as she leaned forward like she meant to launch a full on food fight, Jack caught her arm in his hand. He gently shook his head. She looked into his eyes, fire gone…what's wrong?

"You forgot your clownface," Feliz laughed.

Jack stood, strangely calm, but a forced calm that readied to explode. "The difference between my clownface and yours, Feliz, is that I can wash mine away."

Feliz jumped up and lunged towards Jack, only to be blocked by Candi—who tripped him and then rolled him over her foot so he landed on his back. "Not today!" she snapped with a finger jabbed into his chest.

"Let's just get out of here, Candi," Jack nudged.

And as they walked away, Feliz shouted, "Need your girlfriend to fight your battles?"

Candi started to turn back. "I'm not his-" Jack yanked her arm, tugging her along.

"You're right," Jack said. "Not today. Whatever Plan B is, I'm pretty sure it requires me being on my best behavior. Santa wouldn't listen to me otherwise."

"You can't let him bully you like that."

"How often do I let him?" She frowned…you're right. "But thanks for sticking up for me."

"Jolly Dead Brigade, right?" The Jolly Dead Brigade was their private joke. Their private club! Something they created for just the two of them when they were kids.

On their walk back to the dorms, Jack excused himself to the boys' room so as to get the grits out of his ear. Under the fluorescent lights at the sink, he washed his face, washed out his ear and by the time he was done drying himself off, the mop atop his head was even moppier. He took a good look at himself. "Clownface?" he sniffled. He felt absurdly naked out and about like this.

Candi and Jack crossed the walkway that connected North Pole Headquarters with the older dormitory, briefly pausing to watch the traffic pass beneath them...mostly reindeer-drawn sleds, snowmobiles, and kettle cars—fully automated vehicles that kept the passengers warm around a central fireplace that fueled the ride itself. Around the corner of the dormitory hall a commotion was heard. "Christmas has been uncancelled!" someone shouted. Candi glared at Jack...what did you do? They quickly darted off to the excitement, to where excited elves crowded about. They pushed their way through the crowd to a *RIDE WITH SANTA!* poster, only now it read:

CHRISTMAS UNCANCELLED!
RIDE FOR SANTA!

Candi lamented on Jack's excitement. He snatched the candy cane marker to sign-up. "What do you think you're doing?" Mickie snarled.

"Got as much chance as you," Jack snapped, scribbling his name.

"Ha!"

But then Candi went and did something that not only surprised her, but shocked Jack. She took the marker and signed up, too! "Uh, Candi?"

"There's no chance Santa will pick you before me!" she said.

"What?!" Jack yanked the marker away and scribbled off her name.

"You can't do that!" She snatched the marker back.

"Hey!" And with that, Plan B's obvious requirement for best behavior was shot, for they fought over the marker, yelling like children, both scribbling off the other's name and writing down their own each time they controlled the marker. Fully entertained, the elves cheered, until…Santa came.

"What the devil is going on here?" he shouted. He leaned on his cane, nearly too big for the hall. The elves all scattered so that only Jack and Candi remained, each with a hand on the marker and the scribbled-up poster that had frayed up a bit at the edges.

"Ride for Santa?" he huffed, surprised as anyone. He ripped the poster from the wall and charged away, whacking his cane against a garbage can that made the unfortunate mistake of being in his way. Jack and Candi looked to one another, forgot what they were fighting about, and then chased after Santa back to the Toy Shoppe where rows of elves worked diligently now that it appeared that Christmas had been uncancelled.

In the corner, in a creaking rocking chair, sat Crusty. When standing, he was curiously about twice as tall as other elves, thin and bent with age, sporting a long wispy white beard. He was teaching the young elves how to make basic wooden toys when Santa barged in on the catwalk, rapping the cane against the railing. Work stopped, and Crusty stuck a brass hearing-trumpet to his ear, which helped him hear about every other word. (Crusty just made up the rest.) Candi and Jack rushed in nearby.

With all eyes on him, Santa took a long moment to read the poster before showing it to the elves. "Christmas Uncancelled?!" He looked about the curious, surprised elves, suspiciously pausing on Jack. "Whose bright idea was this?" Everyone looked to one another, but nobody fessed up, believing it was really Santa's idea. "Hear me now," he said. "Christmas is not happening."

Jack stood forward, ignoring Candi's tug at his sleeve to stay back. "It's not yours to cancel, sir."

"Rumpus."

He took another step forward. "We've worked too hard. All year!" Most of the elves looked incredulous at Jack...here we go again. Others, like Mickie, nodded in agreement.

Santa protested. "My leg is-"

"We have hordes of reindeer," Jack interjected. "And we can all chip in and deliver, so it's not like we can't manage." More elves mumbled their agreement.

"It is dangerous."

Jack pointed to the large *Days To Christmas Eve* calendar next to Santa. "We got time to practice." More

26

elves rallied behind Jack. "But when you think on it," he frowned, "don't the reindeer really just fly themselves?"

"The reindeer need," Santa paused. "No! End of discussion."

"Why? Why's that the end of discussion?"

The elves now cheered, much to Santa's surprise. He looked about…what the hell? He mustered up the most blunt and blank expression he could find to drive a threat home to Jack. "Because I am the boss, Rumpus."

"Kids are counting on you," Jack said, and some elves shouted that they wanted to help.

"Jackie…"

But Jack cut him off, starting to chant, "Un. Can. Cel! Un. Can. Cel!" And the elves all started to join in the chant. Some hopped onto their workstations. And Santa sighed, realizing he could be facing a revolt.

Crusty, caught up in the excitement, chanted along with what he heard in the hearing-trumpet. "Rum. Barrels! Rum. Bar-rels!" he chanted, laughing at the fun.

"Fine," groaned Santa, pointing his cane at the dying commotion. "But we do this my way."

And then…a roaring cheer as Christmas was once again, although this time officially, uncancelled. Santa stared at Jack, who turned to Candi with an excited whisper. "I'm going to meet Krampus!"

Although Jack whispered right into her ear, that distance Candi felt between them screamed ever so loud. She felt defeated, dejected, and needing to re-think her next steps.

3 - FLYERS AND HELPERS

Santa worked at his desk, double checking his lists for which kids wanted what toys, and trying to figure out how his new plan might work…or even if it could work at all, when he remembered he had forgot to double check a specific list. An important list. A missing list. He looked for it under papers. A quick check through drawers. He thought he saw some scraps under his desk and crawled underneath to investigate. The Missus entered at that point, reviewing some reports. "All parties accounted for!" she announced, startling Santa, who gave a frustrated grunt when he bumped his head on the underside of the desk. The Missus looked up from the reports and over her reading glasses. "Dear?"

"I reckon this Christmas is gonna be the end of me," Santa moaned, climbing up and rubbing his head.

"From a bump on the head and a broken leg? You've run Christmas Eve with far more complaints than that. Remember the year you had the stomach flu and the Sugarplum Trinkles?" Santa groaned, collapsing into his chair. The Misses paused, trying to read his melancholy. "And you go telling the little ones I cancelled Christmas."

"Had to defer to a higher authority," he smiled.

"Higher authority? Now I know something's troubling you."

Santa pursed his lips together, thinking, and it was in that exact moment when he finally realized why it had been the Year of the Crab, just what had been troubling him, that *something* that he had to do something about. His eyes met hers in a thoughtful embrace. "I'm old."

"Nonsense," she dismissed him with a nod. "Santa doesn't grow old."

"I know I don't look old." He caught his reflection on the computer monitor. "Well, any more ancient than I should. But I feel it." He looked into his reflection a moment, mouth slightly agape, and then made a *tck* noise from his cheek. "Yes," he nodded. "That's what I've been feeling."

She dropped the report onto his desk and sat on his lap, maybe just a little naughty, perhaps suggesting what she might like for Christmas this year. She nodded to the report. "Flyers and Helpers. Whenever you're ready to pass the baton, I'm always with you. We'll grow old…er."

Santa leaned into The Missus for a hug. "I haven't anyone to pass the baton to."

"Maybe one of the Flyers?"

He picked up the list and skimmed it, considering the idea. "Lists, lists and now more lists," he said, shaking the report before tossing it back onto his desk. "Did you give me the Naughty List?"

"I did."

Santa shook his head. "Rumpus."

"Rumpus? Jackie?"

"He was in here. Must have taken it."

She hopped off his lap, began searching about. "Why would he steal the Naughty List?"

"I can't fathom." Santa thought, tapping the end of his nose. "Kinda curious what he's up to, now."

Signaling the end of their shift, the current day on the *Days To Christmas Eve* calendar tore itself off, and grew large as it drifted over the factory floor, finally dissolving into a brief, yet refreshing snowfall. "Teams of two!" Santa boomed, overlooking the crowded Toy Shoppe floor. He leaned on his cane and pointed about with a scroll. "Flyers and Helpers. Flyers deliver. Helpers remain at Mission Control to guide and track. Your first training will also be your tryout. Some of you won't make the cut. Any questions?" The elves remained silent, for even if they had questions, now wasn't the time to ask them. But, of course, they all shared that one burning question…*Is my name on your list?* Santa unfurled a long scroll while putting on his reading glasses. "Jingle will ride. Partner, Winter." Jingle and Winter hopped about, excited to be called. "Angel rides. Partner, Star Cookie." Angel and Star Cookie shrieked, jumping about, holding hands. Santa realized it would take forever to get through his list if he waited for everyone to calm down when a name was read, so he pushed on through the shrieks, shouts, and hopping as he called out Flyer and Helper teams. "Tinsel and Holly. Sugarplum and Ginger. Sunny and Evergreen. Feliz and Mickie."

"Yes!" Mickie fist-pumped the air, turning to Jack. "In your face!"

But Mickie's gloating wasn't to last long, for the next team announced was "Rumpus and Candi." Jack leaned into Mickie's face with wide, happy eyes. "Oh, yea! Ho…ho…ho…"

"Snowball and Pixie," Santa continued, but then was interrupted by Candi.

"Santa? Why am I at Mission Control?" Jack spun to her, glaring. "I know how to fly."

"Because I need you to keep Jackie out of trouble."

Candi looked about as elves giggled. "Can't I ride instead?"

Santa's cheeks pulled up slightly so that his teeth showed. He shook his head. "I don't trust Jackie to keep you out of trouble." The giggles turned into laughter, and Jack's glaring became even more…glaring.

"Well, why send either of us out at all?"

Santa cocked his head askew, put his hands on his hips and paused. "Why did you sign up if you didn't want to go?"

As she began to answer, Jack's goofy eye-threats morphed into a more pleading look. She paused on his wince. "Nevermind, Santa. I'm sorry." Jack was curious, but relieved.

Santa returned to his list. "Buddy with Crumpet." Upon hearing her name, Crumpet began squealing so obnoxiously, it gave everyone a start. Before Santa could continue, he was interrupted, yet again. This time, by Jack.

"Santa?"

"Now what?!"

"Can I have Rudolf?"

"What?" Santa scratched his head, annoyed. "No, you can't have Rudolf! Or any of the other eight."

"Well, who gets Rudolf?"

Santa put his hands back to his hips. "No one gets Rudolf!"

Jack shrugged. "So he'll just be staying at The Pole? Doing nothing?"

Santa returned to his list, dismissing Jack by speaking to the paper scroll in front of him. "If I stay home, my team stays home. Call it a vacation this year." He waved his hand to further dismiss Jack.

"Vacation? From what? What have they been doing all year?"

The Santa Look peered from over the top of the scroll. "Can we please just proceed?" He looked back down. "Noel with Jingles. Swizzle with-"

The next day, the tryouts came. Outside by the reindeer barn, rows of reindeer waited patiently at their sleighs—bridled, in teams of eight, as excited as the elves who were lined up like rows of military awaiting orders and wearing wireless headsets. Santa walked through the ranks of Flyers.

Feliz nudged Jack on the shoulder. "Don't muck this up, Snowflake!"

Some of the elves giggled, but Jack was too excited and anxious to care. He adjusted a pair of steampunk goggles and dismissed Feliz with his standard "Whatever."

Inside North Pole Headquarters, rows of elves sat at computer stations, also wearing wireless headsets. Candi's console showed a radar app in one corner—where a white blip indicated Jack and red blips indicated the other elves. A countdown-to-Christmas Eve app ticked away in another corner. Other random computer background noise filled the remainder of the screen—social media, Solitaire, chat session, and the like. The Missus walked the ranks of Helpers.

"Teams will be sent up in groups of three," she explained. "They will practice takeoff, simulate a near collision, and of course landing."

Outside, Santa instructed the Flyers to check in with Mission Control. "Jack Krumpus, checking in."

"Who?" Candi shot back through the headset.

"Jack. Krumpus."

"Krumpus?"

"Candi…" Jack crouched over his mic, annoyed, as other elves made their way to their sleighs. "Jackie. Rumpus."

"Oh, Jackie! Yes! Jackie Rumpus, proceed to your sleigh."

As Jack walked to his sleigh, Angel was given the clear for takeoff. She took off just as two other riders headed up into the air. Jack climbed into his sleigh, listening to Santa give instruction, growing anxious and bored while watching them go through their exercises. As they finally started to land, Candi told Jack he was clear to takeoff. "What? Yes!"

Inside, Mickie threw a sharp look at Candi. "What are you doing?" he asked. She arched her eyebrows, pretending to not know what he meant. "You just send Jackie up?"

"Psh…no!" she answered with flip of her wrist. She turned back to her monitor to watch the blips, running her fingers through her hair so that it fell like a drape between her and Mickie.

Jack snapped the reins over the backs of his reindeer team. "Woo-hoo!" His sleigh gained speed, approaching the back end of Feliz's sleigh. As Feliz waited to takeoff, he caught sight of Jack approaching, laughing like a mad man. Feliz snapped his team to move out of Jack's way. Now, Jack, thinking that Feliz wasn't going to move, hopped to his feet and pulled his team left. And Feliz, not watching what Jack was doing, also pulled into a left. Collision was still imminent. Ecstatic, Jack pulled right. And, of course, so did Feliz. Surrounding elves started their teams to get out the way, spreading more chaos to ever more teams. Now, everyone was taking off, filling the sky with reindeer, and Santa too busy speaking with Angel and the first two teams to notice.

Noel turned to Swizzle. "Are we just all taking off, now?"

"I guess," Swizzle shrugged. And off they went, two more teams launching. Swizzle passed an elf that was just too intimidated to move, while Noel passed an elf who—no matter how hard he worked—could not get the reindeer to respond to his commands.

As Jack's team nosed in on Feliz's sleigh, Jack laughed and hopped onto the front ledge of his sleigh. He yanked back on the reins, looking like he was trying to stop, but instead called out, "Up, up, and away!"

Inside, Jack's laughter brought the biggest of grins to Candi's face. "Up, up and away?" she asked.

And through the headset she heard, "What do you want me to say?"

"The correct phrase is *dash away all*."

"Then dash away! Dash away! Dash away all!" His laughter was followed by a very cowboy-like "Yee-hah!" Candi's laughter quickly faded into a sad sniffle. Jack was going to leave her after all, and he would be happy to do so.

Jack rode high over the snowy campus, weaving in and out of the reindeer swarm. Some elves laughed. Some gripped the reins in terror. Nobody was as excited or as at-ease as Jack. "Candi! This is amazing! I wish you could see The Pole from up here, underneath the

Lights!" The Lights, he meant, were the Northern Lights, shimmering about them in eerie greenish hues.

"Doesn't Hollyberry Farms look like fireworks in the moonlight?" Jack leaned over the edge of his sleigh to the greenish-blue and red swath that sparkled in the icy landscape—electric, living, undulating.

"Well, look at that!" he said, and then thought a curious thought. "Huh…he says."

And inside, Candi jostled, as if suddenly remembering something and then needing to cover her tracks. "Careful, Jackie! Not sure if your brain knows how to process happy."

Jack laughed, climbed higher, zipping through other flyers. He then dipped down and barnstormed the town—shooting through alley ways and streets, just tapping the top of a kettle car before pulling high up into the sky.

Over by the reindeer barn, Angel and the other two elves looked past Santa, who droned on and on about the most important thing to remember when landing, especially on a rooftop. He asked if any of them had any questions. Angel slowly raised her hand and then pointed to the sky behind him. "Santa?"

Santa turned to where she pointed, and wide-eyed, he gasped, "What the-?"

Among the Helpers, The Missus stopped at Candi's desk when she caught a glimpse of Candi's radar app. "Rumplemints!" she gasped. Candi and Mickie twisted up their faces at one another…language. Evergreen announced that all riders were in the air just as Santa shouted into all headsets, "Abort! Abort!"

"Oh!" The Missus huffed, relieved. "You heard the boss. All riders grounded!" The Helpers all complied, ordering their Flyers to land.

"Land?" Jack grumbled, unsure he heard right. "Already?"

Feliz spied Jack and then turned his flight path into a game of Chicken. Only, Jack didn't accept the challenge. He pulled left, yet Feliz matched him. He pulled right, and Feliz followed. Nearly colliding, Jack and Feliz corkscrewed through each other's teams. "See how you like it, Snowflake!"

Through the headset, Candi yelled at Jack, "What are you doing, Jackie?" She watched the red and white blips spin and dance about one another on her monitor and looked up and outside to the window.

"We've been grounded!" Jack shouted. He pulled up on the tail of their twist, and Feliz climbed back to him—and when they met again, they shot straight up, with their reindeer teams nearly feet-to-feet. Jack turned away and Feliz followed, pulling them into a wide arc. Feliz corkscrewed around Jack, forcing him higher and higher, and then he side-swiped Jack's sleigh to keep him from descending.

At the reindeer barn, Santa surveyed all the landing teams and then looked up high in time to catch Jack returning a side-swipe at Feliz. "Rumpus!" he growled.

Candi threw down her headset and ran to the window, as did Mickie. "No, no, no, no, no," she mumbled; this got carried away fast. Other Helpers crowded around them to watch the dogfight.

Feliz slammed again. "Sick of you, freak!" Jack attempted to pull ahead, but Feliz stayed with him. Finally, Jack bumped his sleigh so hard that Feliz bounced out, shouting as he fell.

Inside, the Helpers let out a collective gasp. Mickie pounded against the glass, "Feliz!"

Jack raced on like some crazy stagecoach driver. "Yee-hah!" But then he saw Feliz's team without their driver. He looked down, spotted Feliz falling, and then dove in a sharp twist. Racing towards Feliz, Jack caught up to him so that Feliz fell next to him. Jack pulled up in a sharp hairpin so that Feliz gently landed into the seat next to him, stunned at the rescue.

"Whoa. Snowflake?"

"It's Jack!" He snapped the reins hard, zipping back up to Feliz's team.

Santa caught the rescue, astonished. "Rumpus!" He knew Jack could fly. He just didn't know he could *fly*. The Missus, absently clutching her blouse near her heart, muttered, "Oi! I really am getting too old for this." The Flyers on the ground and the Helpers inside all cheered, but the spectacle was not over yet!

Jack pulled alongside Feliz's empty sleigh. Feliz stared straight ahead as they approached Gumdrop Mountain through cloud cover. "You gotta land 'em," Jack shouted, but got no response. "Feliz! They'll slam into the mountainside!" Feliz shook his head…ain't moving. "Fine!" Jack hopped to his feet, handed the reins over to Feliz and then leapt over to Feliz's sleigh. But, in his hurry to steer away from the mountain, Feliz pulled away too soon and Jack missed. Feliz gasped at seeing Jack's fail, and stood to see where Jack had fallen.

Everyone on the ground was wide-eyed and tense. "Jackie!" Candi called, and turned to run to help, but The Missus put a reassuring hand on her shoulder. Candi buried her face in her warm embrace. She couldn't watch!

Jack dangled, struggling to pull himself up onto the runner and then up and over the side. He slipped back down. Hanging upside down, he took a look at the mountain coming fast. He pulled himself back up, slid over to the opening, climbed in and plopped into the seat, scrambling for the reins. He pulled the team high, into a loop that corkscrewed out into the opposite direction. "Yee-hah!"

"There's our boy," The Missus laughed, nudging Candi to look as everyone cheered. Well, everyone cheered, except Santa. When Jack finally landed and had slowed to a stop, Santa marched up to him.

"Rumpus! I'll see you in my office!"

Jack grimaced, watching Santa stomp away towards Headquarters. "So much for Plan B."

Flyers and Helpers stood side-by-side next to their workstations. Jack and Candi, however, were missing, having been summoned to Santa's office. "In a moment," The Missus began. "Your computers will display either a Christmas tree or a lump of coal. A tree means you're Flying and Helping. A lump of coal? Well…" She nodded, and the workstations updated.

Elves groaned or cheered. Some elves who received a lump of coal were actually relieved. Still other coal-bearers protested that it wasn't their "screw up" and blamed Jack.

Despite Jack and Candi missing, Candi's workstation showed a tree, but whether they'd remain on the team was what Santa needed to figure out. "Tell me why I should keep you on the team!" he yelled across his desk. "You ruined my training session!"

Plan B. Jack kept in mind, as he weighed his options for a response. *Best behavior.* "Because…" he began. "I gave you…" Santa's frown showed no appreciation for his words. "Opportunities!" he snapped, hopping to his feet. "Opportunities to see things…that you didn't know to look for?" Jack arched his eyebrows, forcing a smile.

"And to think I thought you might actually take this seriously. You knocked Feliz out of the sky!"

"In all fairness, he knocked me first. Plus, I caught him! And then I landed his team!" Jack thought. "I was awesome!"

"Santa?" Candi spoke up. "The fault was mi-"

Jack stunned her by rushing Santa's desk. "No! It was my fault. And I'm sorry. I wasn't paying attention. Pulled the trigger too soon. But I promise you, I am taking this seriously. And I will pay attention Christmas Eve." It wasn't like Jack to simply accept responsibility for something gone wrong…especially when someone else was already willing to do so. Maybe, she thought, maybe Jack was growing up after all.

Santa stared at Jack for a moment. "Did you steal the Naughty List?"

"The Naughty List?" Jack feigned surprise. "Psh…no," he dismissed Santa's question with a wave.

And Santa stared some more, unconvinced, frozen in The Santa Look.

And Jack's nervousness turned him to Candi with a shrug…why would I steal the Naughty List? But Candi's hopes for Jack maturing fizzled, and she stared at him with her own version of a shocked Santa Look with her eyes fixed on Jack's fingers, which he had crossed behind his back.

4 - IMPORTANT THINGS CONSPIRING

"The Naughty List?" Candi gasped, shoving the list back into Jack's chest.

"Shh…" Jack snapped as she looked skittish about.

"You stole the Naughty List," she repeated matter-of-factly, as if it was the only logical thing that could have happened.

"It was an accident," he assured her, but clearly she wasn't assured. "Mostly," he shrugged. "It fell. Into my pocket." He thought. "When I fell off Santa's chair." And then he grimaced. "When I snuck into his office."

"It fell." She rolled her eyes. "Into your pocket." She walked a few paces, until a sigh born out of pressure finally escaped. "Why?"

"Think about it. Krampus is going to go after the bad kids." He shook the list. "To find him, I just need to follow this." She shook her head with a mix of emotion as he tucked the list back inside his shirt. The way she looked at him just now was the same as how everyone else looked at him. "Don't judge me," he snapped. "You're the one who sabotaged me."

"Won't happen again," she grimaced, pacing ahead.

"Why would you do that to me?"

"Jackie, today was the first time in a long, long while that I saw you happy. And it's nice to see you happy. You've got a beautiful, sweet, smile, you know that?"

Jack frowned, "Huh?"

"And I thought maybe it was just because you were going to fly for Santa Christmas Eve." She swallowed, a little teary-eyed. "And maybe it is, but only because you're still bent on running away." Jack felt a little hurt, and a bit confused. Confused about the hurt. Why would he feel hurt? And why would Candi not want him to be happy? "Well, fine. If that is what will make you happy. Go. Run away." She flipped her hands, shooing him away. "Go live with your imaginary friend."

"Krampus is not-"

"I don't care!" she shouted, clenched fists at her sides, startling him. "Just go." She walked away, but then turned back with a pointed finger. "But I'll tell you this, Jackie Rumpus. It will be easier to hate you than it will be to miss you." She paused, starting to cry. "And I don't want to hate you."

Candi…hate him? Candi couldn't hate him. At least, that's what Jack needed to believe. She was probably the only one at The Pole who didn't hate him. And how he hated to see her cry! He crossed his fingers behind his back, putting the other hand up as in a "Scout's Honor" salute. "I promise to come home."

"Don't!" she snapped, still pointing a finger. "Don't make promises you don't intend to keep."

"Seriously. If I don't meet Krampus, I'll come home. And since you think he's imaginary, that's got to be as good as me coming home." He chuckled. And it was the wrong time to be chuckling.

Candi hit him hard on the shoulder. "I'm not a joke," she said, sullen. Jack finally felt that same distance that had been nudging at Candi, and frustrated desperation it brought. He uncrossed his fingers.

"Candi, I promise!"

She kept walking. "Uh-huh."

"Candi! I…I…" He looked about, as if the words he needed were on the floor somewhere. "I perma-swear!"

And that got her attention. Stopped dead in her tracks. She turned back, surprised and suspicious, for a perma-swear is not to be taken lightly…and she doubted he had either the guts or the genuineness to follow through. But he stood there, eyes pleading, his pinky held out as if for a pinky-swear, desperate and expectant. She returned to him, hooking her pinky with his and dared him with a look…go on.

"I, Jackie Rumpus…" he trailed into silence.

"That's what I thought," she said, disappointed and starting to turn away.

"No!" he snapped, his pinky gripping hers tighter. "I'm just thinking what to say. Gotta get the words right. Right?" She frowned…I suppose. "I, Jackie Rumpus, solemnly and permanently swear that if I do not meet Krampus on Christmas Eve, then I will return to The Pole." As he completed his swear, white vapor wisped from their fingertips and swirled about, encasing their hands in ice. The initial jolt of freezing cold simply gave way to astonishment. Candi shook her arm, unsuccessful at freeing her hand, yet satisfied that Jack wouldn't leave her.

"Now what?" she asked.

Jack joined in the shaking. "I dunno. Never done this before!"

After several minutes of shaking, hitting, banging the ice against the wall, and still stuck together, Candi grunted and marched down the hall. Jack struggled to keep up—nearly tripping over himself at times—until she tried to drag him into the girls' restroom.

"I can't go in there!" He clung to the wall.

"I want this thing off me," she insisted, and then started bouncing a little. "Plus, I have to go. Like, really go." She tugged harder.

"Oh!" Jack's eyes grew wide. "No, no, no, no, no." He shook his head, and just to be sure she got the point, added a final, "No."

"Ugh!" she groaned. "Fine!" She yanked him into the boys' restroom and put their ice-encased hands under the faucet. The running water had no effect, except to really make her urge to go, well, more urgent. "What are we going to do?"

Crusty entered and paused on them at the sink, and although they didn't know why, they both felt like guilty children. "Crusty!" they both gasped.

"Ms. Kane?" Crusty said, curious, for it was the boys' room after all. "And Jack Krumpus?"

Jack twisted up his face. "Krumpus?"

"That is the name on your door, eh?" Crusty noticed the ice and chuckled. "Ah! Perma-swear. Something important conspiring?"

Candi said yes, as Jack said no—but then he quickly caught her glance and corrected himself. "I mean, yes."

Candi lifted her hands up for Crusty to see. "How do we undo this?"

"A perma-swear? Oh, no" he clapped. "A perma-swear can't be undone."

"Not the perma-swear," Jack explained. "The ice."

"Oh! Well, that depends." Crusty's deep, sullen, and yet bright and ancient eyes, darted back and forth between them. "Who made the swear?"

"Me."

"Jack, you made a promise to Candi?" Jack nodded. Crusty turned to Candi. "And, Candi, do you accept the terms of the promise?"

"I do."

"Well, now," Crusty clapped again as the ice shimmered and melted. He gave a feeble ho-ho-ho in appreciation to the magic. "The deed is done."

And with that, Candi rushed into a stall and slammed the door. "Thank you!" she called.

Crusty looked about and then down to Jack. "I am in the right place, aren't I?"

That night, as Jack pondered the meaning behind the perma-swear, he grew restless. He didn't want Candi's feelings hurt, but he so did not belong at The Pole…Krampus being real or not. He got out of bed and walked the halls. But it would be okay, he thought. Krampus *is* real. Jack knew he had to be. And Jack had the Naughty List…so he was sure to find his Christmas demon idol. But, what if he couldn't? You can't undo a perma-swear. His wanderings led him out from the dorms; past the rec area, where a few elves shot pool and played ping pong; past the gym, where Mickie spotted for a sweaty Feliz, who groaned as if the weight he pushed from his chest was the most impossible weight to lift; past the cafeteria; past the entrance to the Headquarters offices, which looked positively spooky at night all empty and dark. His wanderings finally found him in the postal area—a long hall, empty and dimly-lit at this hour, flanked by post office boxes floor to ceiling. Jack went to one of the walls, dug into his pocket and pulled out his key. As he reached for the wall, the boxes began to shift—like one of those picture puzzle grids with just one square missing, and you can move just one square at a time to try and create the picture. Boxes slid left, then a column shifted up, boxes slid right, a column dropped down, over and over again until Jack's box landed square in front him. His key shot out of his hand and into the lock. He reached in, pulled out a scroll and was startled to see a pair of eyes looking at him from the other side of his PO box. "Crumpets!"

The owner of those eyes, smiling under thick white bushes, was the Postal Elf. "Jackie? What are you doing up so late?"

"Can't sleep."

"Out for a walk, then."

Jack nodded. "The darkness finds my way." The eyes frowned…okay. "Why are you working so late?"

"This time of year? Desperate kids writing for this or that. Promising they've been good. Plus…Santa finished your assignments."

"Assignments?" The eyes nodded towards the scroll. "Jack opened the long scroll to find two lists—Naughty and then Nice. "Nice?" he winced, thinking. "Snowballs!" He darted off into the dark, the unfurled scroll trailing behind him like a toilet paper tail.

The eyes darted left and right. "Jackie?"

After a long night, the Postal Elf finally emerged from his office tucked behind the PO boxes. But before he could lock the door, a chirping, grinding noise echoed in the far dark. "Hello?" he called, before going to investigate. "Who's there?" As he entered into the dark hall, a pair of red, angry eyes began to glow, followed by more chirping and a sinister, mechanical laugh. He jumped back, but then relaxed as a toy robot waddled into the dim light. He picked up the toy and gave it a look-over. "Curious." It was curious because it was the kind of retro-toy most kids never asked for anymore— the kind of robot that walked and chirped and did little else. It didn't tell the weather. It didn't play games. It didn't even talk. Aside from its glowing eyes, it had a round antenna atop its head that spun as it walked; the kind of scary robot that would scare only movie-goers from the 1950s. It was curious because it was walking the halls alone. Curious, indeed. For Jack used that moment to sneak out of the dark and into the post office. He quickly scrambled inside and dove under a sorting table should the Postal Elf come back, and he did, muttering, "Curious."

The lights flickered on, and the Postal Elf walked right over to where Jack crouched, hiding, and set the toy down on the table just over Jack's head. He hummed as he walked over to a computer and typed in a search for "robot, retro" and looking it over once more added "50s sci-fi." When the search completed, he read aloud, "Randy Jones." And a moment later, "On the Naughty List? Well, that's that then. Maybe next year." He scribbled his notes onto a paper scrap, taped it to the robot, and left Jack in the darkness.

Jack waited a few minutes to be sure the Postal Elf wasn't returning, and once sure, he scurried out from under the table, hit the lights, and got busy. From reviewing his own Naughty List, he had decided he was going to spend his Christmas Eve travelling the United States, specifically the Midwest, and even more specifically, the suburbs of Chicago, starting in a specific town called Algonquin. What he needed to do now was find all the other Flyer and Helper assignments where there would be overlap with his plan, and steal the Naughty kids from anyone Jack might otherwise cross on Christmas Eve.

Sitting at the work table, next to the toy robot, he started with Jingle and Winter's list, working through the Naughty names and trying to figure out roughly where they would be Christmas Eve. "Oh, this is going to take until Christmas Day next year!" he lamented. At the end of it all, he realized Jingle and Winter must be assigned to Iceland, Greenland, and northern Europe. He sighed, trying to figure a faster way to get through all the lists, but the toy robot kept distracting him.

Had the Postal Elf thought to look, he would have found *J.R.* under the right foot. Jack's initials. Jack's toy. Not that he was still in the habit of playing with toys; but this particular toy held bittersweet sentimental value. The robot earned him his Electric Toy – Level One Badge for the Elf Brigade. That summer, he and other elves worked with Crusty learning how to progress their toy-making skills beyond the simpler wooden toys, stuffed toys, and otherwise wholesome fun. At the end of the semester, Crusty's students had to build a simple electric toy to earn their badges. Many chose remote controlled cars and planes. Some chose animated puppies and dolls that could somersault. Hints of Jack's inner darkness came through with his robot project: The Decimator—a retro-futuristic horror that once terrorized kids at the drive-in theaters.

Other elves teased him as he progressed on this final assignment—telling him his robot was "too scary" for kids, and he would never get his badge. But Crusty saw something the other elves didn't. As he reviewed the final projects with the class, Crusty announced, "It's not easy work making dark and scary not so dark and scary." He set the toy in motion across a table top. It waddled, the evil eyes glowed, it laughed its sinister laugh. "And this toy," he proclaimed, "is not so dark and scary." He chuckled in the hoakiness as the antenna atop its head began to spin. Crusty gave Jack the highest marks he could give and handed Jack his badge. Jack had never been so proud. And maybe it was out of jealousy. It could have even been out of fear, for folks tend to fear what is different—whether that difference was a good thing like getting the highest marks possible, or as insignificant having hints of dark in one's personality— but that was the first time Feliz uttered *freak*. And the class laughed, and suddenly, the way they all looked at Jack felt heavier than a look. And Crusty, seeing Jack's happy moment ruined in an instant, turned Jack aside and spoke so that the other elves couldn't hear. "Bright and happy come easy to most elves, Jackie. But some of us have to work for it. And we don't know why. But once we accept that it's okay to have to work for it, the work is much less…work." And Crusty nodded with a wink, sending Jack on his way to ponder his words, calling out, "Good work, Jackie."

Jack touched the toy, standing lifeless and idle on the Postal Elf's table…how ancient it felt. He rolled up Jingle and Winter's list, stuffed it back into the PO box and moved on to Tinsel and Holly. But as he sat back down, and moved the robot out of his way, he had a thought. Randy Jones was on the Naughty List. And the Postal Elf discovered so from the computer. Jack took the list over to the computer and typed in the first name on the list—Elsa Nowak. The computer took a moment and then reported that ten-year old Elsa, from Olsztyn, Poland, most wanted a new computer for Christmas. But Elsa was also on the Naughty List. Jack wished he knew what Elsa had done to earn her lump of coal this year, but that wasn't what he needed to know. She was from Poland, so he could roll up Tinsel and Holly's scroll and move on to the next.

Sunny and Evergreen covered all of Australia. Snowball and Pixie had parts of Africa. Noel and Jingles, South America, along with Sugarplum and Ginger. A search on Miguel Guerro was Jack's first hit in the United States—Sirius and Fornax. He set aside their scroll to continue on his searches. An hour had passed before another hit—Angel and Star Cookie. By the time he had reached the last scroll to search, he could hear the Kitchen Elves in the cafeteria just arriving for the breakfast shift. He had to hurry. When he searched on the name Amy Doohan, he got the final hit—Feliz and Mickie.

"Ugh," Jack groaned. "Why'd it have to be Feliz?" He grabbed the scissors from the worktable caddy and cut off the Naughty portions of the three lists, stuffing them into his shirt. Then he cut off his and Candi's Nice lists and, just as he started cutting it into three parts, he realized that if he cut it into three, he'd have to tape it three times—and using tape is something Jack never could get the hang of. The Wrapping Presents – Level Two Badge forever eluded him. And so Jack made the decision to give all of his Nice kids to the one elf he liked the least—Feliz.

But if taping a box wrapped in festive paper challenged Jack, trying to tape together two scrolls was darn near impossible! "Rumplemints!" Feliz's scroll would try to roll itself shut just as he lined up his Naughty list to the end and reached for a piece of tape from the dispenser. And then, when he thought he had everything in place just right, he'd manage a long piece of tape that would curl and stick to itself before he could stick it to the scrolls. And then he'd have to unstick it from itself, only to have it tangle around his arm. Then he decided to tape each corner of the scrolls to the worktable, but that only caused the scrolls to snap shut, rolling around one another into a tangled mess. And then, trying to get the tape off from the corners, he tore the paper—requiring even more tape to fix it. By the time he was done—he wore tape like all those Elf Brigade badges he had failed to achieve, and Feliz's scroll was taped haphazardly, and a sticky mess covered the work table.

The smell of pancakes and sausage cooking made his belly grumble, reminding him that the Postal Elf would surely return soon enough. He quickly cleaned the worktable, rolled up Feliz's scroll, and climbed the rolling ladder to put it back into Feliz's post office box. But just as he reached into the box, the wall began to move—someone was getting their mail! And whoever it was could hear the faint cries of Jack, as he sped along with his arm stuck in Feliz's post office box—all the way up, all the way over, back to the right, down a few rows, back to the left a few columns, up, over, and when he went all the way down—legs and free arm flinging about—he slammed against the floor and rolled away as the wall continued to shift.

"Oh," he held himself, curled up into a ball around his arm, which stung from getting PO Boxed. But, hearing the keys rattling in the office door, he sprang up, grabbed his toy robot and scroll from the work table and hid, sneaking out behind a tired and weary Postal Elf entering to face another long work day.

The Postal Elf shuffled over to where he had left the Decimator the night before and rubbed his hand over the empty spot that remained…as if maybe he couldn't trust his eyes. He turned about. "Curious."

Jack stumbled into his room, face-planted onto the bed, and immediately started to fall asleep when a knock at the door roused him. "Oh," he groaned. "Go away."

Candi knocked again. "Jackie?" He grumbled, answered the door with half-open eyes. "What have you been up to?" she asked.

He swayed a moment before answering. "What makes you think I've been up to anything?"

To his surprise, she snapped open the scroll with their assignments, cut in half. "Interestingly-"

Jack felt about his shirt, looked about his room. "How'd you get that?"

"We haven't any Nice kids! And you-" She paused to rip a piece of tape stuck to the side of his face. "Never could get your Wrapping Presents badge."

"I got my Wrapping Presents badge."

"Level *Two*," she nudged.

He stopped, shoulders drooping as he shuffled back towards bed. "I never wanted that badge."

She followed him in. "You and tape are not friends." She waited for him to confess his actions, but he ignored her. "Jackie, we have to come up with our flight plan today. How will we do that if half our list is missing?"

Finally, he sat up, looked himself over and tore a piece of tape from his vest, sticking it over Candi's mouth.

"I'm exhausted. I spent all night going over everyone's assignments and looking for overlap."

She peeled the tape from her mouth. "Overlap."

"I'm not focusing on the Nice kids, Candi. Just the Naughty. And I'm only going to the Great Lakes area. Midwest. For whatever reason there seems to be a higher concentration of Naughty kids in the Chicago suburbs. Candi twisted up her face…that's odd. "So I had to take the Naughty kids away from anyone else assigned to that area."

Her head cocked askew. "What did you do with our Nice kids?"

"I re-assigned them," he shrugged.

Over in the cafeteria, Mickie had just sat down to breakfast when Feliz rushed up with their scroll. Both were excited about getting their assignments. Feliz gave it a snap, and it unfurled to an obnoxiously torn and taped list where the Naughty portion was completely missing, only to have been replaced by another section of Nice. Mickie paused, mid-chew, "What do you suppose happened here?"

5 - HAPPY CHRISTMAS EVE!

When the *Days To Christmas Eve* calendar finally tore itself off the last sheet to Christmas Eve, in addition to drizzling snowflakes at the end of the last shift, it shot fireworks over the factory floor. Brilliant, booming, festive, with crazy holiday shapes and animations—like a glowing Santa sleigh charging through a blizzard snowstorm, led by a bright red glow. The elves all cheered, hugged one another for a job well done, and many would get the Christmas party started early by heading over to Thimble's for rounds of peppermint ale. The true party wouldn't start until Christmas Day night, after Santa had returned and had a chance to rest.

With the Helpers and Flyers all chipping in to deliver this year, the pre-tradition tradition got a little muddled. As soon as the cheering died down, Santa appeared on the catwalk, inviting all to a special *Breakfast With Santa.*

Candi slid her tray along the food line in the crowded dining hall, piling her breakfast high—scrambled eggs, pancakes, bacon and sausage…her excitement for the day ahead had her feeling hungry. Not just hungry, but *hungry*…as if a rick of bacon would calm her any. When

Mickie pulled in alongside her and greeted her with "Happy Christmas Eve," she looked at him sideways for only a moment before returning the greeting.

"Happy Christmas Eve, Mickie Rooney," she smiled, keeping her eyes set on the batch of grits being put out.

"Where's your boyfriend?" he chided.

"Where's yours?"

"Oh, burn!" Mickie laughed. "You know what's interesting? Feliz and I have no Naughty kids on our list."

"Really?" Candi frowned. "You don't say."

"I think Jackie mucked things up."

She slid her tray forward, deciding what best to say. Denial? Confess? She had decided that deflecting would be the best course, but then her mouth opened and betrayed her. "What would Jackie want with your list anyway?"

"I never understood what you see in that freak." show

Candi slapped her tray, just hard enough to slip he'd pushed a button. It was a small reward for Mickie, though. Everyone knew Jackie Rumpus was an easy button to push on Candi Kane. She turned away from the food, fire in her cheeks, as she readied to push some buttons herself. But she calmed quick, took a breath. ly "You know, Mickie Rooney, I don't pretend to understand Jackie. But I know this much. He's a true friend. The truest friend I've ever had. And he's kind. And gentle…" She frowned, and added, as if to herself, "Once you get past the harsh." She nodded her thanks to the Kitchen Elf who handed her a small bowl of grits. "He's got a good heart. Which is probably more than I can say for what's standing before me." Then she looked up, nodded. "Happy Christmas Eve, Santa."

"Happy Christmas Eve," he returned. Mickie's eyes grew wide as he turned and looked up at Santa's disapproval. But Mickie got off easy, for Santa's look was all he got. Santa frowned and then took his trays from the Kitchen Elf and went to join The Missus at the head table, where they were joined by Crusty and other elders and teachers. Santa was so preoccupied he barely touched his food, staring off into the space of the room, listening to the background noise of ecstatic elves enjoying each other's company.

"Breakfast is about over, Dear," said The Missus, resting her hand on Crusty's arm as she turned back to Santa. Santa said nothing. "Are you going to make your speech?" Still, nothing. "Well, the least you could do is stop ignoring me."

"I'm not ignoring you," he said, sipping on his coffee. "I don't know what to say. I don't wish to scare them."

She patted him on the back and kissed him on the cheek. "Then don't be scary."

He nibbled some toast, thinking. Most of the elves hadn't ever been away from the North Pole before. And the world could be a scary place, he worried. He panned the room for Jack, finding him looking a bit preoccupied himself alongside Candi. Finally, Santa sighed, stood up and waited for the din of the room to dissipate. "Good morning, everyone." He cleared his throat. "And Happy Christmas Eve."

"Happy Christmas Eve!" the room shouted back, jolting Santa to a smile.

"This year, we're doing Christmas a bit different. And I appreciate the enthusiasm and excitement you all have shown. For all your work in the Toy Shoppe this year, I give thanks." He nodded, and toasted the room with his coffee mug.

"Hear! Hear!" the elves shouted back, clinking their mugs.

"Some of you are going to discover today just how big the world is." His concerned eyes surveyed the room for all his Flyers. "Try to stay out of trouble. It's not just about not being seen. Or avoiding planes. Or being cautious in war zones. You just never know what lurks beyond the chimneys you enter." The rosiness on the elves' cheeks all flushed. Their eyes widened. And, under the table, The Missus kicked Santa's leg. "Oh!" he winced, turning to her with clenched teeth. "My good leg!" She smiled at him as a reminder, with laughter filling the room. He turned back to the elves, pausing in particular on Jack. "Yes, well, what I mean to say is, it's all about the children. Always remember our mission is all about the children."

A few elves picked up on who he spoke to. Feliz leaned over and whispered, "Yeah, Snowflake."

Jack dismissed him with a wave, locking eyes with Santa who continued his speech. Something odd and familiar hit him from those eyes. A darkness maybe? Fear? Worry, for sure. Santa, lately seemed less...Santa-y. Perhaps a bit more like himself? Like, no matter where Santa was, he was always someplace else.

Planning something else? Jack squinted a little, a thought twisting his face...*scheming*.

"First round, check in..." Santa glanced up to a clock. "Three hours. Happy Christmas Eve!"

"Happy Christmas Eve!" the elves shouted. Many stood to take their trays to the tray return, get ready for Flying and Helping, or celebrating at Thimble's.

In the commotion, Jack's thought returned to his mission. He leaned into Candi and whispered, "I have to finish packing."

"Okay," she smiled, and her happiness threw him. Like Santa, she was someplace else. A happy place, but scheming something just as well. "Catch up with me before you leave."

He frowned, "But...I'm leaving...now."

"The Pole, I mean." And as he walked away, she chuckled, "Dork."

Later, Candi waited for Jack at the long windows in the corridor to North Pole Headquarters. She rested her forehead against the cold, refreshing glass, watching the latest round of Flyers launch in the far distance by the reindeer barn. The town below bustled with excitement. The crowd overflowed Thimble's and spilled over to the slightly sketchy Nutcracker Tavern. And with each Flyer taking to the air, the crowds shouted "Hooray!" Kettle Cars zipped here and there, with folks rushing to various celebrations about town. And all the while, Candi watched with an infectious smile. She didn't even care that she wouldn't be able to celebrate this year, being a Helper and all.

Jack tapped her attention back inside. "Candi?" He sounded a bit meek, sad, yet excited. His Santa uniform was standard issue—red with white trim, though the trim was lightly dyed at the ends in shades of purple with black—as if done randomly with markers. Silver diamond studs embossed the black boots, which matched the black belt—also embossed around his skinny frame to where a shiny skull grimaced for a belt buckle. Instead of the Santa hat, Jack went with his elf hat—the one where the bell no longer jingled, but rattled with devil horns. And over his hat rested his steampunk goggles.

Candi took in her Goth Santa and bit her lower lip to contain her smile. "Has Santa seen you?" Jack frowned; shook his head. "You should probably keep it that way." The smile escaped her.

"I'm hoping Krampus will like the nod," Jack smiled back, showing her the devil bells, a little awkward. Then he remembered, and grew excited. "And if this is too subtle-" He opened his jacket to show her his workshop vest with *Krampus* etched across the back. His smile fell back to awkward, but Candi's smile beamed.

"Too subtle?" she huffed.

His eyes arched. "Too much?"

"I don't think so." She adjusted the collar on his jacket. "Got your flight plan all figured out?"

He waved the Naughty List at her and paused, caught between his sadness and excitement. "I guess this is good-bye."

"Uh-huh," she smiled.

"I mean," he swallowed. "For real. For good."

"I know."

Jack didn't know what to make of her smile. "I'm running away. Really." Her laughter baffled him. She laughed, of course, because Krampus wasn't real…just a story to scare Naughty kids into behaving for Christmas. Jack's mouth gaped, his lips quivered as he searched for his words, finally blurting, "I'll miss you."

"I'll see you later."

"Candi?" His confusion on her mood tortured him so.

"You can't undo a perma-swear." She shook her head.

"But I'm going to live with Krampus."

She nodded…uh-huh. But then a seriousness took hold of her look, and she paused, a growing anxiousness in her belly before she finally wrapped her arms around Jack and kissed him. It wasn't one of those Hollywood kisses she had fantasized about for a while now—just a simple kiss. A sweet kiss. A kiss that would let Jack know what they had never before said to one another. That she loved him was obvious. That he loved her, she never doubted. But it was never mentioned. Never acted upon aside from their friendship. That kiss was a line she had decided needed to be crossed in a now-or-never moment such as this. And Jack's wide-eyed surprise and smiling huff, made her beaming smile all the more bright. "Maybe you can't undo a perma-swear, Jackie. But maybe that will give you a reason to *want* to come home."

Jack remained still, watched her skip away towards North Pole Headquarters, her smile turning back to him the brightest thing in his field of vision. His heart fluttered, shocked into happy, yet that made the weight of his sadness all the more heavy. Would this be the last time he would see her? Could their friendship ever be the same if he came back home? Could working alongside his idol, Krampus, ever give him as much joy as he felt in that instant? What was it about him that could take a moment of happy, and twist him into sadness?

He looked outside to the teams taking off. He looked about The Pole, at all the festive elves cheering on the Flyers. To the Kettle Cars zipping along. To the snowy campus mixed with the modern buildings and ancient fantastic cottages.

And a tear fell.

What was so wrong with him? Why didn't he belong here? How could he be so sure he'd belong with Krampus any more or less than he did at The Pole? Why couldn't he just be a happy, festive elf, celebrating with everyone at Nutcracker Tavern? Why couldn't he just be a Nice elf? Or, at least, a good elf?

6 - THE TROUBLE WITH BEING SANTA

Racing his sleigh high on a clear night, Jack descended over the moonlit Lake Michigan, in awe of the Chicago city lights. The rails just skimmed the water's surface, leaving scattering rings in his wake. Jack hopped to his feet, taking in all the cars rushing along a snowy Lake Shore Drive.

"Candi!" he exclaimed, entering into the city and looking up at the skyscrapers. "I never imagined the buildings so big! Bigger than Gumdrop Mountain!" He zipped between buildings, headed for the black John Hancock Tower. "Skinnier than Peppermint Falls!" How the moon and lights shimmered across its glass! "And they sparkle! Like Hollyberry Farms." He twisted away over a rattling el train, and followed along its path. "And trains fly through the city!"

"Jackie," Candi called through the headset, but in his excitement, he couldn't hear her.

Cars bustled along in every direction, heading into the city and out towards the suburbs in twisting, winding roads of golden light. "And cars everywhere."

"Jackie."

He took off his hat and scratched his head, enjoying the cold rush of wind through his black mop. "But if everyone is expecting Santa, why aren't they all snuggled in their beds?"

"JACK!"

"Gah!" He recoiled from his earpiece. "What?"

"Don't forget you're on a mission."

"Right!" He pulled the Naughty List from the Santa sack. "First up…Randy. Randy Jones, you've been naughty." He pulled back on the reins, and his reindeer team pulled the sleigh high into an arc, flying out of the city and rushing towards a much, much quieter suburb that lacked tall buildings and flying trains. But what this town did have was an abundance of holiday spirit. Evergreens were lit up into giant Christmas trees, oak trunks wrapped in blinking mats of light, balls of red and white light dangled from branches, bushes twinkled in every color. Huge blown up Santas waved in the wind, along with Frostys and snow globes. And as Jack descended upon one such festive street, there were plastic candy canes, mangers with plastic glowing Jesus babies, and an army of nutcracker soldiers. One neighbor, apparently in protest, scattered among his yard bright, silver *Festivus* poles.

"Over there!" Jack pointed to Randy's house on the corner, groaning while taking in all the spirited decorating. "Ugh. It's like the Ghost of Christmas Present puked up all over the place."

Candi chuckled. "What?"

"Tacky, Candi…just…tacky." He stood on the seat, leaning over the edge of the sleigh as some white wooden statues of reindeer had grabbed his attention. Some local teens posed them into rather lewd positions, very un-Christmasy, yet making merry just the same. By the time he looked forward again, his reindeer had already begun swirling into the chimney top, like water down a funnel. "Whoa!" he shouted, but it was too late.

Inside Randy's living room was a perfect picture setting for a holiday commercial—stockings hung at the fireplace, a decorated tree in the corner—broad and festive—Christmas-themed knickknacks throughout. You might half expect a crowd of carolers to waltz in, singing about all the wonderful sales they snagged at the local store. But all there was was a grey and black striped cat, who purred and stretched in his sleep. And aside from that, silence that was about to-

POOF!

Red and green flashes of light sparked from the fireplace, where eight tiny reindeer and Jack's sleigh shot out and crashed into the room. The room lost. Horribly. Furniture, knickknacks, and the tree all threw in different directions…waking the cat who screeched, launched like a rocket and landed somewhere in the mess of the tree.

"Ah!" Jack inhaled, eyes darting about. His reindeer waited patiently in their neat little rows. "Huh…he says." One-by-one, three ornaments fell and bounced off Jack's head. His "oh…oh…oh" gave way to a "Yeow!" when the star tumbled down the branches, and poked him in the head.

"Jackie?" Candi called. "You okay, Jackie?"

Jack licked his lips, unsure of what all just happened. "Did you know reindeer can go down the chimney?"

"What did you do?" At North Pole Headquarters, Candi launched an app on her workstation that showed Randy's house from overhead in a thermal heat image. Her eyes shot wide, seeing the reindeer inside the living room. In other rooms, she could see the sleeping kid and his parents…stirring awake. Her breath faltered watching, until after rolling over, tossing and turning, the family all fell back to sleep.

"I wasn't paying attention!" Jack said. "What do I do?"

"Send them back up!"

Jack lightly tapped the reins over their backs. "Uh…dash away all?" The reindeer slowly turned to him with a look that clearly asked Jack if he was nuts. Jack nearly threw off his wireless headset when Candi's suggestion came through that she go and get Santa. "No! Don't get Santa! I promised him I would pay attention."

"You *weren't* paying attention."

"Exactly my problem! Do. Not. Get. Santa!" He huffed. "I know. Kringle it."

"Kringle it?" Candi opened a web browser. "What am I supposed to kringle—reindeer removal?" Mickie turned to her with a curious look, but she was too busy to deal with him. A search engine page opened up on her browser to *Kringle*—where the software developers were clearly from The Pole. She typed in *reindeer removal* and scanned the results. "Removing reindeer poop from boots… reindeer from roofs…reindeer stew? Ah!" She clicked a link. "Removing Rein-," she gasped.

"What?!"

"Oh!" she tapped her forehead, eyes clenched. "Unsee! Unsee! Unsee! That's disgusting. Let's just assume you're the first one ever to land reindeer inside a house."

"Woo-hoo!" came back through the headset.

Candi's eyes narrowed. "Focus, Jackie!"

Inside Randy's living room, Jack unharnessed his reindeer team. "No, that's 'woo-hoo,' I got it! I can't get them back up through the chimney, but I can get them through the front door!"

"They won't fit."

"Two-by-two they won't."

Just as he unharnessed the last of his team, the cat launched from the tree and pounced onto the rump of a reindeer—which then brayed and bucked and stirred all of the other reindeer into a frenzy. They flew. They bounced. They jumped and crashed.

Christmas destroyed the room.

Watching, horrified, as thermal images of the reindeer scattered about, Candi's eyes darted about the app. "Oh, oh, oh!" She covered the app with her hand, winced at Mickie, and then when she peeked under her hand she gasped, "Jackie!" for the ten-year-old Randy finally woke, hearing Jack's commotion from the living room…but Jack was too preoccupied to hear.

Randy yawned and stretched, rolling over, entangled in the blankets of his spaceship bed. His entire room was decorated like a scene from a sci-fi movie. His desk and chair were as if a console from the starship Enterprise. His dresser shaped like a droid, which even lit up and made sounds when its drawers opened. The orange carpet was dotted like some alien terrain, with rock-looking pillows scattered about. The shelves held his prized collection—dozens of his favorite robots— evil and good—from the various galaxies from his favorite movies. Randy sprang up in bed, "Santa!"

Not realizing he earned a spot on the Naughty List this year, Randy was sure this was the year Santa would bring him the Decimator Robot from the 1950s drive-in creature feature *Martian Mutants*. If he got Decimator, he would be happy. Well, his happiness would last at least a week, maybe even two! But then he would really need to get Decimator's robo-sidekick Golan Brink. And then, of course, all of Randy's happiness would depend on him getting that one…last…next…robot. He had to make sure Santa got it right this year; for he asked for the Decimator last year, but received only an original edition droid action figure from a recent flick— still in the package—autographed by the actor who played him in the film.

Randy crawled out of bed and cautiously stumbled down the hall, to where Jack's commotion grew louder. Crashes. Banging. Shattering glass. And then Jack's shout, "Stampede!"

Candi's voice snapped in the headphones. "You've got a kid on your six!"

"My what?"

"Your six. Behind you!"

Jack turned just as a stunned and awed Randy stepped into the room. A reindeer galloped through the air, rounding the corners of the room and briefly paused face-to-face with the child as Jack bounded across the room. "Randy Jones, you've-"

And with that, Randy fainted.

"Snowballs!" Jack shouted. "I didn't get to say my line."

"You've got eight reindeer swarming." On the Kringle page before Candi, a banner animation began. "Don't worry about the line." A pixelated Santa Claus lumbered across the banner, putting presents under the tree. Candi's eyes widened with an idea. "Your sack!"

"What about my sack?"

"Put the reindeer in it!"

Jack snatched the Santa sack from the sleigh. "Brilliant!" He jumped high from the sleigh and latched on to a reindeer's antlers. Pulling the sack over its head, the beast disappeared inside. "Seven to go!"

Just as Candi muttered "Parents on your-" Jack got startled by Randy's dad, who stood at the start of the hall with the mom.

"What the-" The dad surveyed the completely totaled room—furniture and all—amidst swarming reindeer and their child passed out at their feet.

"Ten," Candi continued. Jack could practically hear her head collapse against the desktop.

Jack jumped, palms outward, and pleaded, "Oh would you please just go back to sleep?" And, much to Jack's surprise, a sloshy, glowing snowball shot from each of his palms, smacking the parents dead center on their foreheads in a sparkling, wet blast. They immediately fell to the ground, fast asleep. Astonished, Jack looked at his palms. "Whoa! Candi…did you know we have superpowers outside of The Pole?"

"What?"

Jack had an idea. He turned his palms out onto the mess of a living room. "Undo." And when everything failed to undo, he snapped "Snowballs!" But then, another idea popped. He shot a glowing snowball at one of his swarming reindeer. The one he hit immediately fell asleep, legs outstretched, blissfully and gently tumbling through the air. Jack laughed and began putting them all asleep, hopping across the furniture, throwing glowing snowballs. "Sleep! Sleep! Sleep!" But one excited reindeer dodged a sleep-ball, leaping over Jack, and disappearing down the dark hallway. "Oh, crumpets!"

A few more sleep-balls quieted the living room. Some reindeer had collapsed to the floor, others floated, gently bouncing off each other and against the walls like fuzzy antlered balloons. Jack looked about the room and sighed. "Candi? I lost a reindeer."

Candi scrolled through the thermal app display to see antlers knocking over shelves in Randy's room. "Down the hall. First door on your left."

Jack cautiously stepped into the dark, hearing a noise from behind the first door on his right. "Ollie ollie reindeer, out in free," he called. And as he opened the door, Candi shouted that she said left, not right. A large, blubbering, St. Bernard charged out. Jack screamed, running and stumbling back into the living room. Jack shot a sleep-ball, and the dog collapsed. Momentum dumped him right on top of Jack, who struggled to catch his breath under the weight of the dog.

"Jackie?" Candi asked. "You okay?" But the only response he had was his heavy breathing. "Jackie?"

The heavy breaths stopped, for he clamped his mouth shut, struggling to avoid the drool that dripped over his face. He pushed with hands. Pushed with his legs and as he finally crawled out from underneath the beast, he lamented, "Lamest. Superpower. Ever." He thought his struggles were over, but then the cat leapt out from behind the couch, attacking the devil-bell on Jack's hat. Jack shrieked and spun about, knocking against the wall. "Aw, c'mon!" Finally, he yanked off the hat and flung the cat across the room. Completely disheveled, Jack huffed and puffed and grunted. "Santa can take his job and-"

At North Pole Headquarters, Santa stepped up behind Candi, startling her when he asked, "Everything okay here, Candi?" But, of course, nothing was okay. Jack's meltdown sounded from the headset, telling Santa he could take his job and shove it.

"Rumplemints!" Candi jumped, tightening her shoulders and back. She ripped the headset off and covered the earpiece, wincing as Santa admonished her.

"Language." Santa leaned in and looked at her monitor as she scrambled to close the heat-imaging app. "Jackie having a problem?"

73

"Everything is under control sir. I mean!" She straightened, turning up to him. "We're fine!"

"How many deliveries so far?"

"Uh," she swallowed. "One." Mickie sniggered. "We're still on the first," she said, squinting at how bad that sounded to admit.

"Have him pick up the pace. We've only got tonight."

"Yes, sir." She watched him continue walking down the line, occasionally pausing at other workstations, glancing up at the clock. "Santa says to get a move on."

With no sign left of any rogue reindeer in Randy's living room, Jack heaved the heaviest sigh. "I'm done. I'm done." Over his shoulder the threw the Santa sack, which simply looked as if it were filled with toys—not lumps of coal, or all of Jack's belongings, or a sleigh, or eight tiny reindeer. "Leaving now."

"Did you find the missing reindeer?" Candi asked.

"Yes!"

"Did you remember to put a piece of coal in Randy's stocking?"

Jack opened the door to a cool wind that gusted in on the Christmas disaster—a smashed couch, smashed tables, shattered knickknacks, a broken tree, Randy and his parents collapsed on the floor. Jack's eyes surveyed the mess; his heart twinged with guilt. He'd have to remember to stick the landing better next house. "Let's just say, uh, yeah." He stepped outside and shut the door, but then had the thought that Randy would never know that "Santa" had visited him if he didn't leave a present, or in this case, that lump of coal. How would Randy know to get off the Naughty List? Or, what if he knew he was on the Naughty List and took the destroyed room for his lump of coal? That would be awful; to think you were *that* Naughty that Santa would trash your living room, yet could not even be bothered to leave a lump of coal. He opened the door again and tossed in a coal chunk, quickly slamming the door shut.

The lump of coal tumbled through the mess, as if it tumbled on its own power. The cat watched it hop over the sleeping dog, roll through the shattered picture frames, rebound against the splintered table leg, and finally rest in front of the fireplace. After a brief moment, a lone spark shot out from the fireplace ashes, and was shortly followed by more popcorn-like flashes, which sparked a flame. A fire roared to life. A shimmering portal opened inside the flames. The cat blinked; turned its head askew. Beyond that portal was a hidden world of fire and brimstone; a seemingly endless pit of rock, with flying reingoyles—reindeer with demented gargoyle heads and bat-like wings.

The hairy shadow of Krampus stepped out of the fireplace, with its long horns, goat legs, slithering tail. As it scouted the mess of a room, its long tongue winded out of its mouth and then retreated. The cat screeched, puffed itself up with a hiss, and then fled—bounding over Randy's face to the safety of a bedroom. The sniveling shadow stepped over to the window. Its large, claw-like fingers pulled back the drapes to see Jack tugging reindeer from his sack and reassembling his team. A sinister chuckle slipped loose.

Randy groaned awake, calling Krampus' attention. The shadow took long steps to him, crunching over broken glass as Randy opened his eyes. "Wha-?" He looked the figure before him head-to-toe. "What the hell are you?"

A basket was thrown at him. Randy shrieked. And Krampus' deep, sinister voice boomed, "Randy Jones, you've been naughty." *Naughty* trailed off into a throaty chuckle. Like a Santa sack, Krampus' basket had a seemingly endless interior—dark, with thin beams of light poking in from between the basket slats. Crying children cowered in darkness, but Randy was not ready to accept his fate. He screamed, kicked, pulled, reached out from under the lid—only to have it slammed shut on his fingers and hand. Through the slats, he saw Krampus step into the fire, and fearing he would be burned alive, Randy howled.

But Randy's fate wouldn't end him there, for quickly burning children alive wouldn't serve Krampus' mission. As soon as Krampus' long tail slithered through the flaming portal, the portal shut, and the fire dwindled and died.

Outside, Jack launched his team to get back onto *his* mission, not realizing of course, he nearly just accomplished it with Krampus coming into Randy's house just behind him. "Dash away all!" he shouted, as the reindeer climbed into the night.

A fleeting moment of peace weighed heavy upon Randy's living room.

And then, gentle, chilly white wisps of wind blew in down from the chimney and swirled through the room, which magically began to fix itself. Shattered knickknacks unshattered themselves. The fallen tree unfell, and the ornaments hung themselves where they belonged. The star tumbled upwards, bounding over ornaments and lights, righting itself upon the treetop. Splintered furniture pulled together and sturdied themselves. All things unbroken and unfallen. The wisps swirled past Randy's parents, and they lifted, hovering deadlike back towards their bed. And once they were safely tucked away for the night, the wind reversed itself and whooshed back up the chimney.

Finally, Randy's coal bounced up from the floor, landing in his stocking. And, finally, so it seemed, Christmas gasped a sigh of relief for the havoc it righted in the home of Randy Jones.

7 - LAME!

After narrowly missing Krampus on his very first stop, Jack fell into a rhythm of zipping along from house to house at a proper elf pace. Candi watched the white dot representing Jack on her radar app blip about her monitor screen as she casually snacked on Polar Bearies—chocolate covered hollyberry raisins. She had grown bored, and rested her head in one of her palms, watching that dot blip about….until quite suddenly, the blipping stopped.

"What's the matter, Jackie? Looks like you've slowed down."

In the living room of Jeremy Donner, Jack took off his elf hat and scratched his head, for he too, was growing bored. Restless. Half-heartedly, he tossed a lump of coal into a stocking and sighed, "Jeremy Donner, you've been naughty." He looked about the room, expecting his idol to materialize, and began to wonder how Krampus got about on Christmas Eve. Did he have a sleigh? Did he come down the chimney like Santa? For that matter, where was this world he dragged the Naughty kids to? None of these questions were new to Jack. He had even asked Santa about all his curious thoughts…going so far once to ask Santa if

Krampus was real or just pretend. But Santa would never discuss it, telling Jack he should worry less on Krampus and more on the toys he should have been making.

"Still no Krampus," Jack lamented, shooting up the chimney.

"Duh," Candi said, slurping on a Frosted Moon. Though she was speaking to herself, it irked Jack when she added the sing-song commentary, "He's not real."

But Jack, of course, knew Krampus was real. What he realized, though, was that his plan to meet Krampus was not working. "Can you find out why Jeremy Donner is on the Naughty List?" As he took off high into the sky, Jack scrolled through the Naughty List. He could hear Candi navigate her computer, clicking at keys.

"No-go," she finally answered. "I found the file, but it's password protected." Another long slurp. "You want me to try and hack in?"

"No."

"Why do you want to know what Jeremy's done?" She listened to the silence of Jack staring into the Naughty List, lost in his thoughts. "Jackie?"

Jack hopped up on the seat, excited. Five children, all living in the same cul-de-sac, all on the Naughty List. "Emily, Kevin, Stephen, Mary, and Micha…you've all been naughty." As he shot away towards their homes he laughed, "What did you all do?"

"What are you up to, Jackie?" Candi asked as Jack perched his sleigh on Kevin Mahoney's rooftop.

"Think of it, Candi!" In his excitement, Jack's thoughts were so clear that perhaps he wasn't thinking clearly. "If Krampus is moving around, and I'm moving around, then he's a moving target." He grabbed his sack and then quickly leaped from rooftop to rooftop in the cul-de-sac, disappearing down each chimney before finally stopping in Kevin's basement. "But if I stay still," Jack said, "Krampus will find me!"

"And what makes you think *Krampus* hasn't already paid this kid a visit?" she asked in such a way that Jack could hear the air quotes, cynicism, and sing-song jab.

But Jack paid her no mind. He shook out his Santa sack, dumping five Goth-kids tied to chairs. "Because they're still here." They were all aged between thirteen and fifteen years old. Sobbing Micha was the youngest, had a black mop atop his head like Jack. Kevin was the oldest, whose piercing eyes threw angry glances. Emily, Stephen, and Mary were caught somewhere between the two—moody teens, more fascinated than angry or scared. They all wore makeup, though in different amounts and ways so that they could all be unique while still all being the same—black eyeliner; black lipstick; pierced noses, lips, eyebrows and ears; pale makeup; colorful hair—black, white, purple, dark red, blue— Mary had a mix of colors; and clothes fit for a casual Halloween party. Micha, alone, wore pajamas…and the embarrassment alone was enough to make his eternal sadness even sadder.

"You're not Santa!" Emily snapped. Her short and spiked white hair never moved as she snapped her head. "Who are you?"

"I'm nobody," Jack answered. "Who are you?"

"Emily Dickinson."

Jack frowned. "You're Emily Dickinson?"

"You just quoted her."

"I didn't quote anybody." Jack quickly grew agitated. "You're all on the Naughty List."

Mary chimed in. "What?!" Her long hair faded softly from one dark shade to the next, much like her thoughts. A fluid melancholy. Dark blue blended into deep red, then purple and blackness at the ends, which whipped about as she turned to Kevin. "You said no one would know."

Kevin's angry eyes shot between the kids. "Who squealed?!"

"Shut up!" Jack shouted, taking off his elf hat and scratching the sides of his head. "Shut up, shut up, shut up!" He sighed. "Krampus is supposed to drag you all to Hell. I want to know why."

Micha whimpered. "Krampus? What's Krampus?"

Mary grew sullen. "Hell is empty. All the devils are here."

The others all nodded in agreement. Stephen grew a half-smile, just about as much of a smile as was allowed. "Shakespeare. The dark bard. Very cool."

Jack's eyes grew wide. Having to deal with five different versions of himself was proving to be quite the handful. "Quiet!"

"Was it the lame block party?" Emily asked. "I'll bet it was the lame block party. Freaking poseurs."

Kevin snapped at her, "Can it!" Jack noticed how quickly Emily retreated. As Micha whimpered, Kevin turned his rage on him. "Don't be such an emo."

"I'm not emo," Micha sniffled. "I don't even believe in Santa Claus!"

Jack gasped. "You don't believe in Santa?!"

"I'm Jewish!" Micha cried, and although that should have been enough explanation, the meaning was missed on Jack.

Stephen bobbed his head for air quotes, seeing as how his hands were tied up. "Thought you didn't believe in *organized* religion."

"Conformist," Kevin shot, and with that Jack hopped onto Kevin's lap, looking thoughtfully at him face-to-face.

"You're the boss here, huh? Everyone's afraid of you?" He hopped back down.

"Let me go!" Kevin shook against the rope. "I'll scream for my folks!"

Stephen laughed, and then in his most dramatic, dark tone, added, "A scream. From the abyss of doom. For Mommy and Daddy!" And then his laugher infected Emily, who laughed to tears.

"Scream all you want," Jack said. "Mommy and Daddy are already…asleep." His fingers ticked as he contemplated more sleep-balls.

"Can it, you!" Kevin snapped, and again, Jack noticed how quickly the others responded to his threats.

"Why do you get to make all the rules?" Jack asked, but he didn't wait for an answer. A sleep-ball flashed, knocking Kevin squarely on the forehead. He nodded back, and then the momentum tipped him just enough so that the chair legs slipped out from underneath. Out cold, on his back. The other kids gasped.

Micha sniffed. "You killed him!"

Mary simply looked down at him and observed, "Fascinating."

"Ultimate freedom," Emily gaped.

Jack protested as the kids continued to comment their dark, deathly blackness, until Jack could finally stand no more. "Gah!" he snapped. "No wonder Santa hates me!"

The Goth-kids couldn't make up their mind on whether they were fascinated or horrified that Kevin was dead, and as their bleak-addled banter continued, Jack grew impatient. "Yes!" he finally shouted. "I killed Kevin. Now shut up and tell me about the lame block party before I get really angry!" The teens summarily all rolled their eyes…as-if. But then Jack raised his palm, and the threat of their own sleep-ball death got their attention.

"It was all Kevin's idea!" Emily blurted.

Mary jerked her head to get her long hair from her face. "Our parents made us go to the party. Which was lame."

Stephen explained that their parents all act like best friends, but really can't stand one another.

"Poseurs!" Emily snapped.

Mary sighed. "At least our hate is honest."

Jack stomped his foot and pleaded, "Can we please just get on with it?"

Silence befell the Goth-kids, as their purple and black-rimmed eyes all darted at one another. Finally, Micha blurted out, "We spiked the desserts with diarrhea medicine!"

The white spikes on Emily's head remained stiff, but her shoulders heaved in sudden sorrow. "And then we locked all the little ones inside the bouncy castle."

Mary spoke to the emptiness in front of her. "And when everyone all started getting sick, we locked the porta-potties."

Stephen shed a tear, which left a black trail dripping through the pale make-up on his cheek. "Mrs. Hall yanked on the door. Over and over. And then ran back home. One hand on her mouth; the other on her butt."

"She didn't make it!" Micha sobbed. "She didn't make it home."

Stephen gasped, a memory gripping his throat. "But the kids in the bouncy castle!" The others all looked at him, saddened. "They were still bouncing when it all hit. They tried getting out through the fake windows but ended up deflating the castle."

Micha shook his head. "They had to be peeled out."

Mary stared into the floor. "Some people got lucky." She shook her head, looking up at Jack. "Only some."

More black, drippy streaks from Stephen. "Mostly, it was a mess."

Guilt twisted up Emily's trembling lip. Her bleached-white eyebrows arched up in sorrow. "And then they all started throwing up."

"Horror from both ends!" Micha sobbed.

Emily shook her head. "I never almost felt so bad in my whole life!"

At last, their confession ended, and it wasn't followed by dark lamentations on how the weight of guilt pressed upon their mortal souls, but rather, for a moment, they were simply children. Guilt-ridden children, sobbing their apologies to nobody in particular. These truly repentant kids didn't know what to make of it when Jack chuckled, and then laughed, and finally snorted, and then grew hysterical…crossing his legs, pounding on his thigh. "I'm gonna pee my pants!" he laughed to tears. The Goth-kids looked to one another. They sniffled. Their sobs subsided. Stephen and Mary forced a chuckle or two, and all were bewildered. "That's pretty naughty," Jack said, catching his breath. He thought a moment. "But I don't know if that deserves the wrath of Krampus." He stared at Kevin, still asleep; still believing their secret was a secret that mattered little. "Maybe Naughty means something different to Santa and Krampus?"

8 - ELF ON THE FRIGGING SHELF!

Jack, of course, wasn't the only elf delivering that night. Unlike Jack, and because of Jack, Feliz wasn't delivering coal to any house Christmas Eve…just presents. But something odd struck Feliz at Amy Doohan's house. After spriting about the room, piling presents under the tree, he bounded for the fireplace to find not one, but two stockings—one for Amy, and the other for Sally.

"Amy?" Feliz scratched his head and pulled out his taped-up scroll of Nice kids. "I don't have an Amy," he said. "Just Sally."

"What's that?" Mickie asked through the headset.

"I only brought presents for Sally. We don't have an Amy on the list."

At North Pole Headquarters, Mickie frowned at Candi. "Maybe Amy is on our Naughty List?" Candi caught his frown from a side-glance, and guilt tugged her attention to the opposite direction. She clacked at the keyboard, feigning cluelessness while pretending to be busy. Her stack of crumpled up snack wrappers and empty drink cans had grown, spilling over the edge of her desk and onto the floor.

"We don't have any Naughty kids," Feliz shot back.

"I know we don't have any Naughty kids," Mickie snapped. Candi winced, clacking faster.

Feliz tossed a gift under the tree. "I'm just leaving a present anyway. Gotta keep moving."

"Don't forget the milk and cookies," Mickie reminded him, for that was one of the jobs of the Helpers.

But Feliz hit a wall…a wall of sugar cookie nausea. "Ay-yi-yi. I just can't do another cookie. No wonder Santa's so fat! I'll just take them with me."

"Be sure to leave some crumbs so they know Santa ate the cookies."

"How do crumbs help anything?"

"Look," Mickie said. "Mrs. Claus put it in her notes. It's protocol. Make it look like Santa drank some milk, too."

"Dude," Feliz grumbled. "You know warm milk is the worst? Not taking another sip."

"Just pretend."

"Fine! Could really go for a peppermint ale about now."

"And leave crumbs in the glass."

Feliz hopped onto the couch to get to the cookies and milk that had been left on the end table. "Sheesh!" But, there on the end table, Feliz was greeted by a note for

Santa, held up by Elf On The Shelf. Feliz gasped. "Elf on the frigging shelf!" Feliz snatched the doll. "That is an offensive stereotype!" He throttled the doll, and upon catching his own reflection, gave pause. Taking in his own ridiculous outfit—the elf-sized Santa hat, the elf-sized Santa uniform, the elf-sized Santa boots. A whispered "freak" escaped from him as he dropped the doll. And then a curious anger welled up inside. "I'm an elf on a shelf! I'm a frigging stereotype!"

Jack was right about all of them being freaks. And this gave Feliz a bit of a meltdown. The kind of meltdown that required more than a peppermint ale or two at the Nutcracker Tavern. Upset that he was a frigging stereotype along the likes of Elf On The Shelf, Feliz raided the bathroom drawers for make-up to give Shelfie a make-over. The rosiness of Shelfie's cheeks were paled-over; eyeliner made his eyes angrier, and a thin hoop earring hung from his ear. He etched "Krampus" in black marker across Shelfie's back, and attempted to tear some of his clothes, but when cutting through the pants with toenail scissors, he was met with stuffing that poofed from Shelfie's leg. "Oh, that ain't good," Feliz said. "But not that you don't deserve it." He quickly rummaged the drawers of the bathroom sink and found a sewing kit and then patched him up with a few stitches, but then had the thought that if Jack were to do this he would have made the cut a proper gash. A few shades of eyeshadow fixed that. And when Feliz was done, he looked at Shelfie and thought the only thing that looked out of place was that stereotypical elf smile.

His reflection in the bathroom mirror didn't smile, for it was Shelfie who got the make-over. Feliz still looked like a stereotype. So he took the white powder puff and slowly dragged it across his cheek, smudging away the natural rosiness into an empty canvas. And the dark eyeliner made his eyes as angry as Jack's. And a peculiarly purplish shade of lipstick made his mouth seem like the night; dark, hollow, yet full of endless possibility. He tore a few rips in his red pant legs, and cut a few angry holes in his Santa coat, but smartly avoided giving himself gashes as he had done to Shelfie. When he was done, he perhaps looked like he was ready to pledge the Jolly Dead Brigade. But, of course, the Jolly Dead Brigade had no make-up and dress requirements…membership was about carrying a certain angsty-ness inside one's heart. And, most times, it wasn't even about that.

But as Feliz returned Shelfie to the plate of cookies, and Feliz replaced the note for Santa with a new one that read "Greetings from the Krumpus!" a popcorn spark flashed in the fireplace. Feliz turned to the fireplace, curious. He jumped back as more popcorn flashes bounced here and there until a fire roared to life. And from the flames emerged a dark, shadowy figure.

Krampus!

Jack's idol paused on Feliz, who took in the twisted horns and hairy body. Krampus' face was slightly flat so that his nose was a bull dog snout. One hairy leg was human with a clawed foot; the other was goat-like with a cloven hoof. His long tongue slithered out and flicked the air. "Krampus?!" Feliz gasped, as his right eye twitched and then…he wet himself.

Krampus chuckled, snatching Shelfie in his clawed hand. He turned it over, appreciating Feliz's handiwork.

"Jackie Rumpus," he growled, dropping the "Krumpus" back onto the table and disappearing into the dark of the hall. Feliz stood petrified, breathing shallow.

At North Pole Headquarters, Mickie repeated the word he couldn't believe he had just heard. "Krampus? What do you mean he's real?" And this yanked Candi's attention…what? Mickie shrugged at her, wide-eyed. She slid over to him and yanked his headset aside so that both their heads were painfully wedged in. Feliz uttered a frightened whisper, "He knows Jackie."

Candi bolted upright. The headset snapped against Mickie's temple. He cowered and rubbed the side of his head. "What do you mean he knows Jackie?" she shouted, and all the Helpers on duty turned to her. "This isn't funny, Rooney!"

Feliz hid behind the tree, recoiling from Candi's shouting. "Ay, yi, yi," he whispered. "He's coming!" He drew in a deep breath and held it there, as if doing so would make him invisible, safe.

Krampus strode through the living room, chuckling, as Amy screamed from his handbasket. From the fireplace, a reingoyle poked out from the flames—with its twisted devil horns for antlers, and thin bat-like wings. Krampus paused before it and scolded it like a bad dog. It whimpered from its master's glare and retreated into the fire. Krampus followed after, disappearing into the fireplace before the flames extinguished.

Feliz waited until he could hold his breath no more and then stepped out. His whole body trembled. "I'm done," he said, wheezing a few deep breaths. "I'm done! I'm done! I'm done! I wanna come home!"

"You can't come home," Mickie reminded him. "Kids are counting on you. Santa's counting-"

"I'm coming home." Just then, the white wisps swirled in from the fireplace. "What the-" Ephemeral fog swirled about him. His eyes grew wide. His arms went up. The wind enveloped him, freezing him in a crystalline cocoon before rushing back up into the fireplace. Feliz teetered, slammed forward against the floor and then got sucked up into the chimney along with the Krumpus doll.

9 - SECRET SANTA

Santa, of course, was not about to let the Flyers out into the world without some sort of aid...aid beyond what the Helpers could offer. Normally, the job of minding the giant snow globe in Santa's office went to Crusty. And, normally, Crusty had only one Flyer to mind...and that was Santa Claus himself. This year, with all the Flyers and Helpers out helping, and Santa having nothing to do, the globe was watched by Santa...who watched over his Flyers with a fierce gaze.

Santa sat before the giant snow globe, watching Feliz's scene play out in Amy Doohan's living room. His index finger, pressed against the glass, commanded the white wisps of wind through the ephemeral fog. And, just then, the white wisps that unfell and unbroke and froze things in cocoons, retreated into Santa's fingers. As the last of the wisps disappeared, and Amy's living room was left pristine, with no sign of Feliz or the Krumpus doll, Santa paused and sighed in disappointment.

"Snowballs," he grumbled. He turned to the list of Flyers on his desk and crossed off Feliz's name. Only Jack, at the top of the list, remained. Now, mind you, none of the other Flyers had the experience of wetting themselves hysterical after meeting Krampus; nor did they make the unfortunate mistakes that caused Christmas to destroy living rooms, but as Santa had watched throughout the night, he found subtle reasons to worry that something was missing in all his Flyers. Something special. And, despite all his flaws, Santa was realizing that this special quality—whatever it was—was not lacking in Jack. He rapped his fingers against the list and then got up, bumping into The Missus as he exited his office. "Can you send a team to the barn?" he asked her. "Feliz's team should be arriving shortly."

Mrs. Claus nodded. "Where are you headed?"

"Infirmary. This was a bad idea."

She called to him as he walked away. "Is Feliz okay?"

"Aye," he nodded, never looking back. "He will be."

At his workstation, Mickie panicked. "Feliz?" he called. His Flyer had stopped responding, and according to the protocols set forth by Mrs. Claus, the appropriate response was to not panic. "Feliz!" He and Candi turned to one another, frightened.

Candi checked the radar app on her workstation. Jack hadn't moved any. "Jackie?" She waited for as long as she could stand, but that wasn't very long. "JACK!"

Jack winced and recoiled. "Would you please stop shouting?"

"I need you to come home," she said.

"What? Why?"

"Krampus is real!"

"Duh," Jack smiled, adding a little sing-song jab himself.

"No, I mean he's really real!"

He couldn't understand the urgency in her voice. "I know!"

"Rumplemints, Jackie! He knows who you are!"

The thought of Krampus, his idol, knowing who he was, made Jack feel all sorts of proud. "Krampus knows me?!"

"That doesn't sound like a good thing, Rumpus!"

Jack winced again. "Shouting…"

Candi paced, tensing up—frustrated. She finally threw down her headset, clenching her fists. "Crumpets!"

To which, the unfortunately-named Crumpet turned from her workstation. "Yep?"

"No, crumpets! Not Crumpet. Crumpets!"

As she stormed away, Mickie called, "Where are you going?"

"Uh…" she paused, "biobreak. Be right back." But Candi knew she wasn't going to be right back. She had to keep Jack from meeting Krampus.

Santa chatted with the Elf Nurse in the bright-white clinic. "Feliz Navidad," he nodded. "Should be arriving shortly." And with that, a red and green light poofed in the fireplace. Still encased in ice, Feliz shot out and slid across the room, spinning until stopped by Santa's boot.

The ice quickly melted as Feliz started screaming, hysterical. "Feliz!" Santa called. "Feliz, Fel-" Frustrated, Santa hit him with a sleep-ball, and sighed, thinking while tapping the end of his nose. "Keep him out 'til morning." He left, but turned back in the doorway, crinching up his nose as if smelling something disgusting. "Oh, and you might want to get him out of those clothes."

Santa thumped through the halls of Headquarters, hobbling with his cane clicking against the floor, mumbling to himself some curse about being too old. The clicking cane stopped at Candi's unmanned workstation. Santa blinked, as if half-expecting that the blinks would magically make her appear. He turned to Mickie, who sat, staring off into the windows to the cold snowy night. Twiddling his thumbs.

"Where's Candi?" Santa asked, giving Mickie a start.

"Bathroom. I think." And he thought. "Been awhile."

"Any updates on Jackie?" Mickie shrugged. "And what are you doing?"

Mickie looked about, as if he were being accused of doing *some*thing. "Nothing," he insisted. "I didn't know what to do."

Santa put his hands to his hips. "But sitting there…doing nothing. That seems like the right thing?"

"I don't. Um…" Mickie's eyes darted left and right. "What should I do?"

An annoyed sigh followed The Santa Look, which was missed on Mickie. "Nothing, Mickie," Santa grumbled as he clicked away. "Just keep doing what you're doing."

Mickie watched him huff away, then dutifully returned to doing nothing. The snowflakes tumbled down outside, and Mickie's mind wandered out the windows and up, and up, and up, to where snow became snow and perhaps had not even begun to fall just yet.

Candi, on the other hand, had no time for a wandering mind. She speed-walked through the hallway, startled upon hearing Feliz shrieking in the distance. She raced away outside, rushing past the Kettle Cars that zipped along, hiding from the crowd outside Thimble's, past the edge of town and out to the reindeer barn. Once there, she grabbed a familiar brown saddle and went straight to Rudolf's pen. Rudolf was so happy and surprised to see her, his nose glowed. He was a full grown reindeer, a bit gray in the muzzle from age, but still had as much energy as any. Candi threw the saddle over his back, patted him along his sides. "Okay, Rudy…just like always, but faster." He grunted as she tightened the belt. "Jack's gonna meet Krampus." More grunts. He stomped his foot. "What do you mean, so?" She raced around to face him. "If they meet, the perma-swear means nothing." She shook her head. "He won't come home." He nudged her just as the barn doors threw open and elves led Feliz's reindeer team inside. "Oh! Shh…" She ducked down at his side and realized something. "You knew Krampus is real?" she whispered.

"Any idea what happened to Feliz?" one of the elves asked.

Rudolf brayed, moved uneasy. "Shh…" Candi whispered, calming him. "Rudy, your nose!" As the elves approached, she quickly covered his glowing nose with her hand.

"Not a clue," said the other elf. "I heard something about Krumpus, but-"

"Can't imagine him and Jackie going at it again on Christmas Eve!"

"Exactly!"

Suddenly, the barn doors threw open again and the wind rushed in. A red streak shot high into the night. The elves turned back to the doors, Feliz's reindeer uneasy.

"What was that?"

The second elf went to the doors, looked out into the cold with a shrug. "Probably just the wind."

That red streak, of course, was Rudolf and Candi, shooting higher and higher into the night, to where snow became snow, and hovered so delicately before letting its grip slip. They dashed over land. And dashed over ocean. Over cities and lakes, cars, and the suburban tackiness that was Christmas. Candi leaned in to urge Rudolf on faster. "Homestretch, Rudy!" she shouted. "Everything you got!" And the red streak brayed, and shot faster over the Midwest skies.

10 - WISHES REALLY DO COME TRUE!

It didn't take long for Jack to realize the flaw in his new plan of sitting around and waiting for Krampus to find him…it was all the sitting around and all the waiting. He fought off boredom by building a model of the reindeer barn on the bar top. The kids all watched in awe as his hands moved, rapid-fire, twisting cocktail napkins, straws, toothpicks and other random items into something amazing. The finished model wasn't red, but was otherwise a pretty accurate representation of an old and weathered barn that couldn't possibly house hordes of reindeer.

Kevin groaned back to life.

"Hey!" Micha looked down on Kevin, speaking to Jack. "Mister."

"Jack," he nodded back, checking to see if the detail on north side of the barn was right.

"Mister Jack. Kevin isn't dead."

"Undead bliss," Mary commented.

Emily considered, "A vampire?"

The thought of any one of them, especially Kevin, being a vampire should have been ridiculous, let alone a bit terrifying, but Stephen couldn't contain his excitement at the thought. "A vampire?! Cool!" And then he remembered how uncool it was to find something so cool. "I mean," he shrugged. "Whatever."

Jack sighed, turning the kind of look to the Goth kids that Santa usually held for Jack…The Santa Look…are you possibly that stupid? "I just put him to sleep is all," he shrugged.

Micha's eyes were raw from sobbing—not the kind of cry that elvish ears can't tolerate, but a whimpering sob. "I want to go home."

"Sorry," Jack said, and he truly was sorry. "We just have to wait."

"For what?"

Kevin jerked awake. "Get me off my back, you hobbit!" Jack hopped off the bar stool, and in a sing-song tone suggested the Goth leader say please. "I'll please kick your-" But before Kevin finished his sentence, Jack rocked him upright and stood upon Kevin's knees.

"You're not very nice," Jack observed.

"Who asked you?"

"Emily Dickinson," Jack snapped, but just as he headed into an unfinished sentence of his own, popcorn sparks upstairs yanked his attention. A fire glowed at the top of the stairs and then…a shadow! Jack was all grins—as if his beaming smile took hold of his whole self, and its happiness overwhelmed his body. He hopped up and down upon Kevin's knees. "He's here! He's here!" he exclaimed, his voice shaking.

Kevin looked up. "Who's here?"

"Krampus!" Jack's idol was mere feet from him. His Christmas wish of many years, finally coming true! He trembled. A squeak escaped his throat as his fought off a scream, nearly passing out from the pressure in his neck. And then…he all-out fangirled.

And, of course, finding anything so cool, was just so very uncool for Stephen. "Get a grip, man."

In her monotone drab, Emily confessed how she fangirled once. "When I met Andy from Black Veiled Brides. I got all tangled up in my cloak. Knocked over both of us."

"I'm embarrassed for you," Stephen said.

"Then security tackled us. Broke my nose." And then, as if it were a crowning achievement, she added, "I bled all over Andy from Black Veiled Brides. Ruined my cloak, though."

Krampus' legs stepped down onto the stairway, and Jack paused. He was about to meet his idol. And he didn't want his idol to see him fan-girling. Why…everyone probably fan-girls when they meet Krampus, he thought. He had to calm down, get it together, be cool. "Be cool," he said to himself, and then—poof!—he disappeared behind the bar.

The kids watched Krampus descend, and when they got a load of his full form, a towering dark creature in the basement, they got their freak on. At first, Jack thought they, too, were fan-girling, but it wasn't an excited scream. Jack's excitement blinded him to their terror. All but Kevin tried to scoot away, stuck in their seats, so that Kevin sat silent and alone.

"Kevin Mahoney," Krampus growled. "You've been naughty." The children all screamed as Krampus swooped up Kevin—chair and all—and stuffed him into his basket. And to Krampus' surprise, standing in Kevin's space, was Jack, smiling bright. "Jackie Rumpus?" Krampus crooked his neck. "You've been naughty."

And Krampus surprised Jack with a chuckle, swiping for him. "What?!" Jack shouted, hopping away in time. Krampus' empty fist knocked over Emily and Stephen, who were KO'ed, down for the count, out like lights— and not at all in the sleep-ball sense. Krampus had hit them hard. "No!" Jack shouted. "Don't hurt them!"

"You're coming with me!" Another swipe and a miss. Micha's sobs quieted as he and Mary were knocked out as well. Jack paused on their limp forms, heartbroken.

"No!" he shouted at his idol. "Not like this!"

"Oh? You say."

"I want to help you!"

"Krampus doesn't need help."

"But I can get the bad kids for you." Jack surveyed the bodies, keeping one eye on Krampus. "Like these. And you don't have to hurt them."

"Only need Kevin Mahoney," Krampus stepped forward, causing Jack to take a few steps back. "And I didn't need you to get him." Krampus swiped for him, missed, and smashed the reindeer barn.

Jack looked at its ruins, pained and realizing, "I really am on your Naughty List."

High above the cul-de-sac, Candi descended, pointing to where Jack's team perched upon the rooftop of Kevin's house. "Over there!" she pointed. Rudolf dove, and as they neared the house, Candi added "We're going in!" But in all the years Rudolf had flown with Santa, "going in" was never a thing…they always landed on top of the house…why would they ever go inside with Santa? The reindeer objected, locked his legs and tried to put all the stops on. "Relax," Candi said, rubbing his neck. "Jackie says it can be done." And as Rudolf skidded through the air, he swirled into the chimney sideways.

And Candi and Rudolf found themselves spinning through Hell—Krampus' domain. Fire, flying reingoyles, trolls way down below on the rocky cliffs. Candi gripped tighter in fear, and on one of their spins about, managed to catch a glimpse of a fireplace burning up above. "Up, Rudy!" she shouted. Rudolf managed to still the spinning, shook off the dizzy, and shot up to the fireplace.

Poof! Candi and Rudolf tumbled out of the fireplace, still burning with Krampus' open portal. Candi flew off the reindeer and knocked over the flat screen tv. Rudolf, meanwhile, rolled into a sofa table and shattered family photos and knickknacks. Candi rubbed her head, nauseous. "Oh, that did not feel good." She helped Rudolf to his feet, rubbing his sides. "Are you okay, Rudy?" A loud crash from the basement startled her.

And that crash was actually a smash, as Krampus kept swinging for Jack and missing. Jack hopped from the bar top. Smash! He hopped onto the sofa. Smash! "But I wanted to run away with you!" Jack shouted, hopping onto the end table. "Be your helper." Smash! He realized why Santa never delivered on his wish. And he realized he misplaced his idolization. And he felt angry, and hurt, and betrayed by his own heavy heart. "You were my hero!" he sniffled.

And this caught Krampus' attention. He stopped. Dropped the basket. "Hero?"

Jack caught his breath, realizing the absurdity of his wish. "I wanted to come live with you." Krampus cocked his head skew and thought. His long tongue flickered out, went up his nose and cleaned out snot, thoroughly grossing out Jack. "That's just," Jack swallowed. "Oh, nasty."

"You can show me where the North Pole is."

"The Pole?" Jack wiped away a tear. "You don't know where it is?"

"Polar Magic," Krampus thought. "Confounds it." And it almost looked as though Krampus had calmed into someone Jack could like. Someone thoughtful. With purpose. A mission and a reason.

But when Kevin struggled inside the basket, Krampus kicked the basket across the room. "Quiet!" he shouted, and the viciousness of the action weighed on Jack. He lamented on the other kids, passed out from their blows.

"W-why do you want to find The Pole?"

Krampus spat. "Because Christmas should be mine!" He jutted his face into Jack's, so that Jack tumbled backwards. And then, Krampus smiled, seeing Candi running down the stairs. He rushed to retrieve his basket.

"Jackie!" she called.

"Candi Kane!" Krampus growled, hurrying up the stairs and stuffing her into his basket before she could realize what was happening. She shrieked as he added, "You've been naughty!"

"Jackie!" she cried.

And Jack bounded to his feet and up the stairs. "Candi!"

Candi tumbled out of the basket, scurrying away across the living room floor. Krampus chased after, pausing when Jack lobbed a sleep-ball at him. When it had no effect, Jack lobbed a barrage of sleep balls—all of which had a similar no-effect except to annoy Krampus as a glowing-sparkly-wet mess bounced off him and piled about his feet.

"Weak Polar Magic," Krampus chuckled.

"Do something else," Candi suggested, climbing onto Rudolf's back, to which Jack shouted that he didn't know what else to do. Rudolf's nose glowed so bright, filling the room red and blinding Krampus. He charged, head-butting Krampus to the gut. Krampus threw back, smashing into the fireplace and destroying the mantle—pictures, stockings, knickknacks all scattered. Her grip gave, and Candi tumbled up and over Rudolf's head, bouncing off Krampus and onto the floor.

Krampus shook off the blow, snarled, and retreated back into the fireplace.

Jack and Candi breathed a moment of rest, and just as they thought they had won, Krampus reached through the flames and grabbed Candi by the ankle.

"Jackie!" she shouted. And she scrawled and kicked, but was yanked and dragged backwards into the flames. Jack dove to her and just missed. They scrambled to lock hands. "Jackie!" she shouted again.

Her screams faded into the flames.

The flames faded into dark.

"Candi!" he called, aghast, taking in a few bated breaths. He looked about. A few more breaths. What to do, what to do?! He climbed to his feet and surveyed the fireplace. "Open sesame?" Nothing. "Grus vom Krampus?!" More nothing only agitated him. "Krampusnacht! Krampuskarten! Krampus schnapps!" He stomped, kicked, punched and finally screamed a blood-curdling yell, collapsing onto the floor in tears. His Christmas wish, his only Christmas wish, the one Christmas wish for this year and many years before…took away his Candi. It was his fault, he sobbed, too overwhelmed to hear Rudolf scratching his hoof on the floor and sniffling for attention.

Rudolf let him cry it out for a moment before gently nudging his cold nose against Jack's neck. Jack coughed to stifle his cries, took in the beast, and appreciated the comfort. He scratched Rudolf's muzzle, and freak-to-freak, he sniffled, "Hey, freak." And the freak's nose glowed soft and dim, giving Jack an idea.

Santa!

Jack rushed into the kitchen, frantically rummaging through drawers until he finally found what was needed—a pen, a pad of paper, and an envelope. The chair legs at the table squealed, and he hopped up, standing on the chair and speaking as he wrote:

Dear Santa,

Every year, we get one Christmas wish. Just one. And every year you never come through. It's your fault that I-

"Gah!" he grimaced at his own words, tearing off the sheet from the pad, crumpling it and tossing it away. Gotta be good, he thought. Gotta be good. He tugged at his hair and thought.

Dear Santa,

I know that every year I wish for the same thing, and you never give me what I ask for. And I know that this must sound like I am asking you for the same thing again. But it's different. I need your help. Krampus took Candi! Please open the door to Krampus so I can get her back. I've been a good elf this year.

He thought, swallowed, and finally erased his last sentence. Santa would know the truth.

I've been mostly a good elf.

And again, he thought and erased. And sorrowful tears welled up and trickled down. Why was it so hard for him to be just a regular, jolly elf? Why did he hate The Pole so much? Did he really hate The Pole? Or, did The Pole hate him? The cold, he hated. Making toys, red and green, his stupid elf name, Feliz Navidad and

Mickie Rooney. All these thoughts he pondered as he wrote what finally felt honest.

I'm sorry I'm such a bad elf. Please help me anyway.

Tearful, he stuffed the letter into the envelope and scribbled: Santa Claus, North Pole, URGENT! Into the cold outside he trekked, leaving tiny footprints on top of the new snow, to the mailbox at the end of the driveway. As soon as he shut the door on his letter, a brilliant puff of light knocked him onto his back and shot the letter high into the sky with a sparkly trail.

11 - DUNKLESTIMMA

A gleeful Krampus bounded down a rocky path that had sprung from the other side of Kevin's fireplace. To one side was a cliff wall, and to the other a sheer drop. Horrid creatures screeched and howled in the vast, fire-filled, space. A few dead or slowly-dying trees dotted the landscape, which was barren save for the many scattered broken and lost toys.

The inside of Krampus' basket was cramped and dark, not quite of the same sort of magic as Santa's sack, though it still held more space inside than it appeared to on the outside. Hands and feet squirmed and pushed and kicked, and children cried out for their moms and dads. An occasional hand or leg poked outside of the basked, only to get slammed shut upon.

At last, Krampus arrived to a jail he had built into the rock, and which was guarded by a troll that had bull dog teeth, thick matted hair, tiny horns, and hairy fawn legs. The child prisoners scattered into the darkness of the cave when Krampus ripped open the barred gate, tossed in a tumbling heap of children and slammed shut the door. Even though the children cowered, cried and sobbed, the only sounds that emerged came from the newcomers—who tumbled over one another and struggled to their feet. Candi sprang from the new pile and charged the gate…the only one brave enough to do so.

"Where to now, Krampus?!" she spat. "Gonna get your jolly on by kidnapping more kids?" She looked about the dirt and soot-covered rock walls. The children all cowered, except for Kevin. He stood, also looking about, taking in his new surroundings with a mix of fascination and justified concern, absently untangling himself from rope and smashed chair bits from around his limbs. He approached the bars, paying no attention to either Krampus or Candi, feeling the bars and their odd coldness in the heat of the place, and to himself he muttered, "The devils are all really here."

Now that he was back in his space, Krampus felt more relaxed. He moved slowly, jutting and angling as his movements held thought and purpose. "We all have our role in this Christmas pageant, Candi Kane," he said, eerily calm. And he and the elf locked eyes with one another, sizing up the bigness and smallness of one another, before he raised a calm and human hand to the space before him. His eyes rolled up, expectant, and then turned back on Candi. "Dunkelstimma," he whispered.

Candi's eyes went wide. She spun, slapping her hand over Kevin's mouth, so that they both tumbled. And a wispy darkness emerged from the newcomers' mouths, smoking and swirling and tumbling into a shadow-ball that rolled through the air to hover at Krampus' palm. Krampus looked at it, fascinated despite it being something he witnessed time and time again, year after year, and he grimaced a gleeful smile as silence gripped all the newcomers. The shadow-ball rose, higher and higher, and merged with a much larger shadow-ball that sounded of nonsense cries and agony. An occasional shape emerged, not unlike a hand, or a face, but only something that was *merely* like a hand or a face—grabbing and shouting.

Krampus' gaze turned back from the large shadow-ball back to the cell, and he surveyed the frightened eyes before him. "Terror grips the harshest soul," he said. "It's raging silence takes them home."

Candi charged the bars again. "Jackie won't leave me here!"

Krampus thrust his face into the bars in a vicious threat. The children all scurried back so that Candi and Kevin, alone, remained. Unmoved. "I'm counting on it!" Krampus shouted, reaching through and yanking her into the bars by the collar. "And you best learn some manners, elf. Pity the spell passes you."

Candi groaned at the pain, but then gasped when Kevin did the most unexpected thing. He placed a hand on Krampus' arm. "Mr. Krampus, sir?" Kevin swallowed, looking about. "I want to home, please."

Krampus turned to Kevin and chuckled in his surprise. "And you, too? See that, Candi Kane? Kevin wants to go home, *please*." Krampus sighed, and released his grip on Candi as if realizing he had let his temper get the best of him. And although Krampus was a demon, and not a man, his demeanor changed to that of a gentleman. "You, Kevin, are a quick study. Wants to go home, *please*, at that. You just might go home soon enough." He turned to the troll guarding the jail. "Fetch us a cuppa tea, might you? While we wait for her friends."

The troll scampered as Krampus bounded away.

Candi and Kevin looked to one another, curious. Candi twisted up her face, not believing what she had just heard. "Did he just say fix us a cuppa-"

"Tea," Kevin nodded. "Yes."

12 - LETTERS TO SANTA

Santa hobbled through the halls of Headquarters, occasionally rapping his cane against random obstacles in frustration—a garbage can, a copier, a stack of paper reams that some bored elf had stacked into the shape of a Christmas tree. The Postal Elf stepped in his path and nearly got whacked with the cane as he stepped between Santa and a Frosted Moon vending machine.

"Ah!" he shouted, cowering from the cane so fast he tripped and fell to the floor.

To which Santa reeled back and gave an "Oh, ho!" Santa caught his bearings and helped his friend to his feet, apologizing all the while and brushing away chocolate remnants of a haphazardly-eaten Polar Bearie. He looked at the melted chocolate in his palm and wiped it off against his sleeve. And after making sure the Postal Elf was indeed as fine as he insisted, he noticed the letter. "What's this?" he took the envelope and turned it over. "Nobody writes me Christmas Eve."

The Postal Elf wrapped a bony finger around the envelope to point out, "Marked urgent. Most curious."

Santa opened it and read, and with a heavy sigh revealed its author. "Rumpus." He thought a moment, tapping his finger against his nose.

"Do you need me to help?"

"No, no," Santa said. "You're overdue for a break." He patted the Postal Elf on the shoulder as he walked on. "Why don't you join the party over at the Nutcracker?" He hobbled along, more thoughtful now, and surprisingly less frustrated. But the problem that had been haunting him for so long had returned. He was tired. But, being Santa, there was no room for being tired. Krampus took Candi? And Jack finally met his idol. He must be scared out of his wits, he thought. Them meeting wasn't supposed to happen like this.

Santa made his way down a long hallway, dim and empty with row after row of empty cubicles. The elves had all finished their jobs for the year and were off—celebrating at Thimble's, resting at home, or Flying and Helping. At the end of the hallway he turned to an old entrance for the old Workshop—back when the Workshop and Headquarters shared the same small space. It was a bit of a museum nowadays. He stepped through the space, remembering making toys, the smell of sweat and pine sawdust, how big and magical everything felt, and yet how simple Christmas used to be back in the day. He reached the far end of the Workshop, and creaked open an old and heavy wooden door to the outside and stepped into the snow and cold. The wind blew through his clothes as he stepped along a flagstone path to an ancient cottage. Light from the fireplace inside shimmered in widening swaths onto the snowdrifts below the windows.

Santa stepped up to another large and ancient wooden door and tugged on a rope that jingled a bell inside. And he waited, rubbing his hands on his arms for warmth, wishing he had detoured to get his coat. He jingled the bell again and knocked until the door finally creaked open and Crusty's tired eyes peered outside.

"Santa?" he exclaimed, opening the door wide and ushering him in from the cold.

"Oh, good!" Santa stepped inside, stomping snow off his one shoe into the mat that cheerily welcomed visitors to *Make a Wish*. "You're awake."

"Of course, I'm awake," Crusty said, though he was dressed for bed, wearing his robe and a long striped night cap. "It's Christmas Eve," he added, as if Santa might have forgotten.

"I need you to mind the globe."

"Bring my robe?" Crusty asked, as if it were the silliest request, spinning about and looking for it, forgetting that he was already wearing it. "Bring my robe. My robe." He repeated, still circling and searching.

"It's…um…" Santa started to indicate that the robe was about Crusty's shoulders, but instead just corrected the confusion. "No, not your robe. The globe. I need you to mind the globe."

"Oh?!" Crusty wobbled, a bit dizzy from the spinning. "Thought we weren't doing that this year?"

"Change of plans," he said, and the tiredness melted his cold face. Crusty watched him, thoughtful, two pairs of ancient eyes staring into each other.

"Getting to be your time, is it?"

"I reckon so," Santa lamented, swallowing.

"Well," Crusty smiled wide and his eyes brightened, perhaps the only one at The Pole who could understand what had been bothering Santa all this time. "There's no shame in that." He pointed a bony finger to the space between them and then turned to an old and ornate cupboard covered in wood carvings of a forest scene— an older Santa, a different Santa, with a giant sack of toys being pulled by a team of four horses; and riding alongside him was Krampus carrying a switch and a basket; both of them looking merry. An old, weathered, green felt cap with fur trim and holly berries hung from a hook on the side. Crusty reached inside the cupboard and pulled out a bottle of Nog's Menthe Rum from 1892. "We should be celebrating!"

"No, Crusty. No celebrating. No time tonight."

Crusty paused, put the bottle back and looked at his longtime friend. He dragged a small stepstool before Santa and nudged him to help him up so they stood eye-to-eye. "If I had any magic left in me," he swallowed. "I'd grant just one last wish." He patted Santa on the shoulder. "That you could remember all those letters you've answered and all those wishes you've granted, all the joy and hope and Holiday Spirit you've brought to all those children all these many years and…" He trailed off, thinking back to all his own many years, and then added, "And find happiness there."

Santa thought, and a smile slowly emerged. It was a sad smile, but for both of them it would do. And, strangely enough, the tiredness was gone, replaced with a smoldering fierceness whose embers got stoked. "Oh,

Crusty. I think there's more magic left in you than you realize. Mind the globe, old friend?"

Crusty nodded. "Turn, you whippersnapper!" Santa complied, and Crusty hopped on for a piggy-back ride back into Headquarters. Crusty rocked side-to-side as Santa hobbled, rushing through the halls towards his office.

"Divvy up Feliz's list between Angel and Sirius." Santa pointed to an imaginary list that hovered in the air before him. "Have them move double-time."

"Double-time, check."

"Hone in on Rumpus. If Krampus runs loose and off the handle, call all Flyers in."

"What about delivering all the toys?"

"One bridge at a time." They reached Santa's office, and Santa helped Crusty climb down. He nodded a thanks and a good-bye and as he turned away, Crusty called him back.

"Tell Krampus I said hey."

And to Santa, that was the oddest request. "He's not the Krampus you once knew, Crusty."

"And you're not the Santa he once knew. Tell him Crusty would like to share some biscuits. Over tea."

Santa twisted up his face as he rushed on, and muttered to himself, "Okay…" He marched down the hall with such force his cast crumbled off. He threw aside his cane as the elves cleared a path. He strode, determined, towards the glass doors to the outside. He pulled on his black leather boots, threw on his Santa-jacket, wrapped himself up in his thick, black leather belt. He turned to the full-length mirror and checked himself out. Those embers fully stoked, roared alive and he looked fierce…I AM SANTA!

He turned to leave, and as the automatic doors opened and the cold wind rushed in, The Missus called him back, "Oi! Kringle!"

Santa hopped to a stop and turned. The doors shut. The fire faded.

"Forgetting something?" she asked.

Santa's eyes darted about, and he patted himself down—had his belt, his gloves, his boots…what could he be forgetting? Ah! Of course! he realized, and he kissed The Missus goodbye.

"I meant your hat," she said. She tugged the hat over his head and fixed the puff ball just so. "Where would you be without me?"

"Lost." Santa smiled.

"Hopelessly lost," she playfully jabbed him, kissing him. "Bring 'em home."

"Wish me luck."

She smiled with a wink and nudged him on, but Santa hesitated. "Keep an eye on Crusty, eh? He's a little-" He gestured with a wave of the palm…uneven.

"Go. Go," she urged him along.

117

13 – THE SLIPPERY SLOPE OF KRAMPUS

Elves, known for making toys, are creative types capable of making the most outrageous things imaginable. In Jack's case, in this particular moment, he was creating the most outrageous mess in Kevin's kitchen. He scoured the drawers and cabinets, pulling out things in search of what he needed. The junk drawer looked as if it had all but exploded—with empty pens, unsharpened pencils, paper clips, long expired pizza coupons, rubber bands, dried-up glue sticks, and empty rolls of gift wrapping tape all thrown about across the counter tops and floor.

But Jack finally found what he had been looking for…a roll of duct tape.

Now, it was well known that Jack and tape of any sort were not friends, as Candi would say, and duct tape was a particular nemesis, for it was particularly sticky. He carefully peeled back a corner, and then just an inch or two and thoughtfully attached it to the counter top so that he could safely unroll a long band of tape. So far, not so bad, he thought. But when he tore the piece from the roll, the tape stuck to his hand. And when he tried to peel it off with his other hand, the ribbon began to stick to itself in one, two, and then three places. And when Jack tugged at it to get it straight again, the part sticking to the countertop unstuck itself and the tape curled on itself and Jack, and he tangled himself in it as if it were some sticky python. He tripped and fell to the floor.

"Snowballs!"

It took several attempts, and several face-plants to the floor, but Jack finally managed it…he created a sash out of duct tape, that draped from his shoulder across his chest like a frighteningly unelegant Miss America, bearing Rambo-style a steak knife, a two-pronged fork, a wooden ladle, and bamboo skewers. Had he fallen just the right way, his mission would have ended fast, and in a most horrible fashion. But, he didn't fall, and still he searched the kitchen for weapons of any sort he could find. A frying pan could hurt, he thought, but was too heavy and bulky, especially being of the cast iron kind. But then, a knife block caught his attention. So much so that he didn't notice a red and green poof of light from the living room. Santa's here.

Jack reached for the largest knife from the block, appreciating its possibilities. In Jack's tiny Elf hands, the knife looked like some small sword. It was a vegetable knife, the kind you might use for carving a turkey, not realizing it was really for veggies. He scraped it against the honing rod, imagining its use as he swung it about.

In the living room, Santa surveyed the mess, putting his palm to his head and grumbling…oi. He crunched over some smashed knickknacks to pet Rudolf on the head. Christmas was definitely destroying living rooms this year. His cheeks puffed out as he sighed, crunching over more knickknacks as he made his way to the kitchen. Jack swung about the large knife, doing battle against an imaginary foe. Santa stepped into the kitchen and softly called out, "Rumpus?"

Startled, Jack spun about, pointing the business end of the knife at Santa. Jack. Was. Pissed. His eyebrows furled. The rosiness of his cheeks burned through nearly as bright as Rudolf's nose.

"Santa?!" Jack relaxed, recognizing the intruder. "You're here?"

Santa looked at the sharpness pointed at him. The part of him that felt like a dad to all the elves and children about the world weighed on his heart. "Of course, I'm here."

Jack looked at his knife. His teary eyes darted to the floor. "He's got Candi."

"What's with the get-up?" Santa asked, trying to lighten the moment, but Jack wasn't ready for anything light.

"It's all my fault," Jack said, shaking his head. "He took her."

"You going to shish-kebob Krampus?"

Another nudge for lightness from Santa only brought out a viciousness from Jack the likes of which Santa had never seen. "He's got Candi!" he seethed, gripping ever tighter about the knife's handle.

Santa bit his bottom lip, weighing the moment, taking in the overwhelming hurt on Jack's face, the kind of hurt that pretends to be angry. He got down onto one knee, gentle and fatherly. "And we'll get her back," he reassured Jack, taking the knife and placing his hand on the back of Jack's shoulder. "But this isn't how we do things."

"He's evil," Jack cried. "Candi was right. He's really evil."

Santa carefully lifted the sash from Jack, appreciating its ingenuity. And it's desperation. "Wasn't always so," he said, wrapping his palm around Jack's cheek, at once trying to comfort and instruct. "And I reckon there's still a part of him that isn't so evil. But, Jackie…" Santa swallowed, sighed again. "You can't match evil for evil. That's a slipperier slope you can't fathom." Jack nodded, conceding and sorrowful. Their eyes locked until Santa's darted towards a pair of feet that poked out from behind the kitchen island. Santa rose, cocked his head aside and side-stepped to glance at Kevin's parents…collapsed in a heap. "Huh," he swallowed. "He says."

"Sleep-balls," Jack grimaced.

"I gave you that magic to fix the reindeer stampede!"

Jack frowned, and his head pulled back. "You saw that?!" To which, Santa shot his Santa Look…duh. Jack sucked through his teeth, suddenly feeling ashamed, though he didn't know why. "Is there a recommended dose? I really had to juice them up." His palm went to his eyes to massage his temples. "A few times."

"Ah," Santa sighed. "They'll feel like they've had a few too many peppermint ales." He looked about the kitchen. "When they finally wake up."

"Seriously, Santa." Jack shook his head. "That is the lamest superpower ever. Except maybe for Aquaman."

Santa's eyes arched, as his upper lip pulled aside from beneath his beard. "Well, thankfully, your superpower wears off come sun up." He looked about and then called up to the ceiling, "Crusty?! A little help?"

Jack looked about as well…Crusty? And then, familiar white wisps called upon from a giant snow globe in Santa's office swirled in and about from the fireplace. The shattered pictures and knickknacks shimmered and rose about Rudolf, who marveled and brayed and stomped as he had never seen this particular magic before, watching everything become unbroken and unfallen, finding their rightful place on the mantle and end tables that fixed themselves. The ephemeral fog that filled in the space about Rudolf tumbled and swirled into the basement, bringing sounds of the unbroken, unfallen and un-stomped as wisps swirled into the kitchen and wrapped about Jack.

"What the-?" he exclaimed, amazed as the kitchen cleaned itself. He jumped back when Kevin's parents lifted up off the floor, hovering and dead-like, with their arms drooped and their hands dragging along the floor as they floated back towards their bedroom. Jack's eyes shot wide as he stepped toward the doorway to the living room to watch them fade into the darkness of the hall. He turned back to the kitchen to see the tape, dried-out glue sticks and expired pizza coupons shoot back into the junk drawer.

"Jackie Roland Rumpus!" Santa shouted, jolting Jack from his amazement. Four sleeping children, still tied to chairs, floated up from the basement and into the living room.

"I needed Krampus to find me!" Jack explained, though the stern look from Santa let him know his explanation wasn't satisfactory. "It seemed like a good idea at the time!" Santa frowned and glared. "I'm…" Jack's heart felt heavy. The children tumbled in the air, their binds untying themselves, slipping from their chairs and floating out the opening front door back to their homes and beds. "I'm so-"

"I know!" Santa snapped. "You're sorry!" He bared his teeth, shaking his head just slightly. "You're always sorry."

Jack stepped up to Santa. "But this time I'm-"

"Really sorry? Yeah, you never learn!" Santa stepped past Jack to survey the kitchen.

Jack looked up to the ceiling. "Crusty!" he called. "Make sure they're okay?!" His eyes darted about, half-expecting Crusty to materialize somewhere in the ceiling. "Krampus knocked them hard. Like, really hard." Jack turned to Santa. "Crusty can do that, right?" A shameful glare from Santa is like the most angry, admonishing look from the most angry, admonishing dad. A gust of wind blew into Jack's face and mussed his hair as the wisps swirled and rushed backwards up into the fireplace…up into Crusty's fingertip that pressed against the snow globe in Santa's office.

Crusty watched the last of the wisps retreat into his fingertip, taking a curious, appreciative look at his finger. His eyes wandered about the long office, to all the books, and the piles of letters stacked and bound like old newspapers, outside to the Christmas Eve night, to the faraway mountains where Santa's telescope peered. He took an old black-felt top hat from a shelf and put it on his head, and felt a little bit like he was Santa Claus. "Time," he said, tapping against the top of the hat, "marches forward." He turned back to the ephemeral fog inside the globe.

Jack stammered, chasing after Santa—dodging the side glances and wringing his hands. Santa searched through each cabinet, slamming each door shut as he moved on to the next.

"I'm-" Jack paused, interjecting upon himself before Santa could add another "I'm sorry." "I *am* sorry," he sighed. "I'm sorry I'm such a bad elf."

"Jackie!" Santa slammed a cabinet shut. "You're not a bad elf. You just do naughty things." He moved on to the next cabinet. "Nine times out of ten, given the choice between doing the naughty thing or the doing the nice thing, I'd wager you'd do the nice thing." Jack's eyes grew wide, having never realized that Santa felt this way about him…really?! But Jack's elation fell flat as Santa snapped, "But in the most naughty way conceivable!"

"I-I-I don't," he stammered. "I don't think I-"

Santa finally found what he was looking for…a cylinder of salt…and he stomped towards the living room, pausing just long enough for his shoulders to tense up. His hands rose and throttled an imaginary neck in front of him. "You kidnapped four children today!"

"Five," Jack said matter-of-factly. "Technically." He grimaced. "If I'm being honest."

Santa stopped in front of the fireplace and turned back to Jack. "And who else do we know that kidnaps children Christmas Eve?"

"It wasn't like that! I mean!" Jack thought…it was just to get Krampus to find him. It wasn't mean. It wasn't kidnapping! But, yet it was…just like Krampus! "It was just supposed to-" And then Jack realized just how much he behaved like his former idol this Christmas year. "It was just-" He tried to explain himself. To excuse himself! But as he stammered to find the words, the only two that managed their way past his lips were, "Oh! Poop!"

"Yeah," Santa nodded, bending down towards his most troublesome elf. "Poop." He sprouted back up and turned his frustration at Rudolf, who nibbled at the tree.

"That's why you hate me?" Jack asked.

"Candi," Santa said. "Would you say she's bad?" Jack's face twisted up. The thought would never have occurred to him…Candi, bad? Santa nodded, "Reckon she's been joyriding Rudolf." Jack was aghast. His eyes widened at the realization, connecting dots as Santa used his boot clear a space around the fireplace. "And I thought it was you!"

"Candi got Christmas cancelled?"

"And I gather she got it uncancelled, too." He kicked away a present that had been ever so neatly wrapped in a gold foil and red bow. "You see," he said, "you just do whatever pops into your head—complete disregard for naughty or nice. She, on the other hand, considers the difference, but does the naughty thing anyway." And then he turned on Jack, shooting a look that made Jack realize something he hadn't quite ever realized before. "For you, I might add."

"For me?" Getting Christmas uncancelled, knowing how Hollyberry Farms glistened in the moonlight, sabotaging his training, the perma-swear…

Santa poured a salt line around the hearth, and then closed his eyes as he turned his face up to the ceiling. "She must be the naughtiest elf ever! I can only imagine Krampus' excitement when *she* showed up. And yet, she's one of my favorites. So, Jackie." Santa turned on Jackie, looking down upon him, leaning his face into Jack's, and poking Jack in the chest as he enunciated each word. "I. Don't. Hate you." He sprang up straight. "Rudolf!" Rudolf turned, mid-chew, with glistening tinsel-strands hanging from the side of his mouth as he munched upon a branch. An ornament that looked like a popular cartoon character swung from the end of the branch. "Stop eating the tree. That can't be good for you." Santa tugged at the branch, double checking it. "This thing even real?" Rudolf gave another cautious chew before returning to the tree. Santa reached up and took the star from the treetop. He threw it down to the floor, inside the salt line, and stomped and ground it to pieces with his heel. Finally satisfied that the star bits were fine enough, he clapped, turned to the fireplace and sized it up. "Now. Candi." He closed his eyes, turned his palms out, and calmly uttered, "Krampusnacht."

Jack climbed onto the end table and sat, waiting for something more than nothing. But nothing happened. Santa remained still, palms out, eyes closed. The fireplace remained cold and dark. Jack glanced back and forth between the two. "Tried that," he finally said.

Santa shook an annoyed hand at him. "There's more to it," he insisted. "Been awhile."

"Bu-"

And now two annoyed hands shook at Jack. "Bu-buh-buh-buh-buh…hush. I'm thinking." Jack bit his bottom lip, as if to keep the rest of his words trapped inside. And Santa thought. "Krampusnacht steht vor der tür," he began at last, his eyes growing cloudy and gray. "mit schalter und korb. Krampusnacht steht vor der tür." He trailed off, lips quivering as if to start a word but being cautious that the right word was being started. And, finally confident he had found the words deep in the nooks and crannies of his mind, his eyes grew wide, and he pointed at the fireplace. "böse kinder fürchten."

Impatience swung Jack's legs about. "All that just to open a door?"

"Hush, you." Popcorn flashes bounced about Santa, who hopped back as the fireplace roared to life.

The heat and glare made Jack pull back, excitement glistening on his rosy cheeks. "What are we gonna do?"

Santa pointed into the flames. "I am going to go in there and get Candi." And then he pointed to the end table. "You are going to stay with Rudolf."

"What?!" Jack protested, hopping to his feet. "No! I want to help!" His fists clenched dramatically in front of his chest as he dramatically emphasized, "I *need* to help!"

"Too dangerous, Jackie. Once I go in, Polar Magic will be useless."

"Which is a roundabout way of saying you really, really need me."

"Jackie, no. I can't do what I need to do and worry about you, too." Jack, of course, started to protest even more, but Santa cut him off with a pointed finger. "Promise me. Stay with Rudolf."

"Okay," Jack caved, but not before crossing his fingers behind his back.

And from The Santa Look came, "I mean it, Jackie."

"Uh-huh," he nodded.

Frustrated, Santa grabbed Jack's arm and shook it to show he wasn't fooled. "No more games, Rumpus!"

"Fine," he sighed, pouting. "I'll stay with Rudolf."

Although doubtful, Santa cautiously turned back to the fireplace. "Wish me luck." A red and green aura shimmered as he stepped over the salt and into the flames.

"Santa?" Jack cocked his head askew. How strange it was to see Santa bent in the flames, yet not burning as he looked back at Jack. "Thought your leg was broken."

Santa feigned surprise. "It's a Christmas miracle!" He touched his finger to his nose, nodded with a wink, and vanished.

Jack stared into the fire. He thought he could see the shadow of Santa darting about somewhere behind the flames. With an unbroken leg. Candi was perhaps the naughtiest elf ever? For him, no less? And he was as wrong about Santa hating him as everyone else was wrong about Jack hating Santa. This night wasn't supposed to go like this, he thought, and yet the more he thought on it, losing himself to the flickering light, he suspected it couldn't have gone any other way.

14 - MAKE LIKE AN ELF

The Naughty children had accepted their fate. Crying was useless. Screaming was hollow. They were in Hell, on Christmas Eve no less. Nobody was going to help them. Candi and Kevin, on the other hand, were furious with sweat—climbing the bars, tugging on the bars, shaking the bars, and occasionally throttling the bars as if choking the life out the demon who dragged them there—looking for any kind of weakness. But they weren't going anywhere any time soon. For that wasn't how Krampus operated his Christmas Eve.

Kevin turned to the other kids. "C'mon!" he urged. "Help us!"

Sullen eyes looked back at him with hardly a movement. Just then, the strangest thing happened. Candi stopped testing the bars. She let go, slapping her hands over her pointy ears as she fell to the ground. She winced in pain and her eyes twitched, searching for the source of the painful noise. An eight year old girl stood in the center of the cave. Her long blond hair hid her face, but it was obvious that unlike the other kids, her tears weren't silent. She sobbed. She howled. And, well, she cried the kind of tantrum cry an eight year old might cry finding herself locked in a cave in Hell. On

Christmas Eve. Her name was Amy, the girl whose stocking belonged to Feliz's missing Naughty list.

"Oh, please don't cry," Candi pleaded, approaching Amy like one might a cornered badger—with extreme caution and perhaps wondering why you might be approaching such a mongrel in the first place. Still, she tried to comfort the girl, touching her forearm. "Crying kids is like the worst sound to an elf." Amy's cries escalated, as did Candi's wincing...unlike her attempt at comforting, which all but abated. "Seriously, kid! Nails on a chalkboard." Several of the other Naughty kids shuddered at the thought. Candi looked about...what to do, what to do? "Gah!" she gasped at another loud outburst from Amy. Her hands slapped back over her ears. "I know!" She rushed to the bars and spied a broken doll. "Kevin? Can you reach that?"

Kevin knelt down and stretched his arms through the bars, fingers reaching, further, and further, as if he could will them to grow. But, just as he was about to reach the broken plaything, he pulled back and looked at Candi. "Wait a minute! Why's she crying?"

"I want my mommy!" the girl shrieked, causing Candi to double-over as if punched to the gut.

"But she's crying. And why can I talk?" Silently-crying Naughty kids all looked to Kevin.

"Doll first," Candi winced. "Please?" As soon as Kevin had the doll, Candi snatched it and gave it to Amy, with a not-so-comforting pleading grin of desperation. Amy hugged the doll, sniffled and quieted, and Candi's shoulders drooped as she began to relax. But then Amy took a look at the doll—it's broken arm, singed hair and burnt dress, missing an eye, and covered in dirt and soot. She threw it down, horrified.

"It don't even have a eye!" she shouted, crying again.

"O. M. G!" Candi snapped, covering her ears again. "I really am in Hell."

Krampus' shadow ball descended and hovered in front of the cave before entering, mesmerizing everyone as it seeped through the bars and breaking apart like a hand of swirling, menacing fingers. As it headed for Amy, Candi dove at the girl and slapped her hand over Amy's mouth. Still, Amy jerked and a darkness emerged, oozing between Candi's fingers before launching, wisping, swirling into the shadow ball. Though still crying, Amy fell silent once again.

"That didn't happen with me," Kevin observed.

"Well," Candi thought. "The silence is…better?"

Kevin looked at Amy, and then about to the other terrified Naughty kids. "Imagine screaming for help, but you can't make a sound."

And suddenly Candi felt awful, despite Amy subjecting her to one of the worst sounds to an elf. "Oh," she said, simply, reaching out to touch Amy's forearm again.

Kevin frowned as he thought. "Raging silence takes them home."

"What's that?" Candi asked.

"What Krampus said. Raging silence takes them home."

"Speaking of which…" Candi nodded, and they returned to the furious task of searching the bars for any weaknesses. And again, they kicked, and they tugged, and they sweat, and they throttled for a time. After one particular throttling, Kevin cried out a primal grunt through gritted teeth and gave the bars a kick and a punch, hardly reacting to the pain in his knuckles. Candi had climbed to the top, looking for loose connections between the bars and the cave wall. She paused on his grunt, and slid down to meet him eye-level. Something was bothering him, she thought, beyond the obvious problems they faced. He palmed his sweaty hair out of his face, catching his breath, and looking to Candi's eyes. "Krampus wanted only me. Why just me?"

"Who knows why he does what he does?" she shrugged.

"But…I'm the only kid who can talk here. Why just me?"

"Because I slapped your mouth shut?"

Kevin nodded towards Amy, who listed silently in the center of the cave. Tears streaking the soot on her cheeks. "Didn't work on her," he said, giving the bars another shake and another angry grunt. He turned his back to the bar and slid down as his resolve diminished. "It's hopeless. I must belong here."

Candi watched him slide down, frowning. "Don't say that!" She slid down to him. "It's never hopeless. Jackie thought he belonged here, too. But he was wrong. And you're wrong. Unless…" She turned about, towards all the hopeless faces of the silent Naughty kids. "Unless, you're right. And you really do belong here."

133

"Gee, thanks."

"No, I mean…" She grew excited. "What if that's the point? You don't belong here because you realize that you do belong here." It wasn't quite The Santa Look that he shot at her, but it was a look of confusion, as if he couldn't process what seemed stupid to him. Candi understood the look, having given one similar to Jack on countless occasions. "It's about penance," she explained. "Remorse. And you must be feeling guilty about something." She turned to Amy, pointing. "And you! What if you're an ungrateful brat?" Amy's eyes grew wide, distraught. "No! No!" Candi insisted, rushing over to pat Amy on the hand. "I'm not saying you are…but what if that's why you're here? You got your voice back, but then rejected the doll because she doesn't have an eye? And then poof!" She looked about the Naughty kids, who all looked thoughtful back at her. "What would all of you do differently so Krampus wouldn't bring you here?" And as they all reflected, wisps of dark shot back into the cell and into the children's mouths. They all gasped as their voices hit them. "See that, Kevin! It's never hopeless." She smiled, slapping him on his knee. "Now make like an elf and help me." He briefly considered her outstretched hand before smiling and reaching back.

Just then, Santa peered from around the side. And Santa, not knowing that Candi had already fixed one of the next problems on his to-do list when helping the Naughty kids find their voices, lost all element of surprise as the children charged the bars calling out "Santa!" Such happiness and joy! "Santa!" For this year he wasn't just the jolly old elf to bring them presents…he was their savior. "Santa!" Oi, he thought, urging and pleading for them to quiet.

Somewhere high up above, at the end of a dusty cliff path, burned a fire from the wrong side of a fireplace…Kevin's fireplace. And in Kevin's living room, Jack paced about as Rudolf feasted upon the tree. Were Jack like any other elf, say Mickie, being told by Santa to stay put and do nothing would have found Jack staying put and doing exactly nothing until he was told to do something otherwise. But, as we know, Jack wasn't like all the other elves. His impatience grew as wild as his imagination…wondering what could be happening to Candi…that it was all his fault…that he made this stupid wish year after year…that- "Gah!" He stomped off to the kitchen.

And Rudolf, who had been minding his own business and munching on the Christmas tree, stopped mid-chew, and turned towards Jack's departure. More tinsel strands hung from the sides of his mouth, glistening with the firelight. When Jack returned, determined, gripping the knife and wearing his weapon-sash, Rudolf protested. He grunted and stomped his foot.

"I know what Santa said," Jack insisted, stepping around the reindeer. "But-"

More grunts came from the beast, along with a fierce red glow.

"How is doing a nice thing naughty?" Jack charged into the flames, and Rudolf bowed down after him, biting onto the sash and dragging him back. Tangled in the tape, Jack lifted off the floor, feet kicking, until the tape finally tore and he tumbled to the ashes and burning embers. Jack seethed, on all fours…the only heat he felt was his own rage until he spied something sparkling in the ashes. He reached for it, almost hypnotic. "Huh…he says." He crawled back out of the flames, standing up to show Rudolf. "Candi's necklace."

A jack-o-lantern bat made festive with a Santa hat.

"I made her this." Rudolf's nose dimmed. Jack thought back, swallowed as his heart grew heavy. "Right after I failed getting my Wrapping Badge. My last chance." He looked into Rudolf's dark eyes. "Too many failed badges. Got kicked out of the Elf Brigade." He sniffled. "I acted like I didn't care, but Candi knew. I just wanted to belong to something. Anything. Who needs the Elf Brigade, she said." His eyes lost to the memory. "We'll be our own brigade. Just us. The Jolly Dead Brigade. I made her this. And she gave me-," Jack held up the candy-striped ring that only fit the middle finger of his right hand. "Oh!" he said, quickly retreating his hand as he realized he was giving Rudolf the bird. "She's everything good about The Pole, Rudolf. Everything good to me, anyway. I have to get her back."

A grunt. A brief, red glow, and Jack got the message.

"For a freak with tinsel hanging out of his mouth, you're pretty sharp." Jack tugged the tinsel free, a little disgusted as the strands slipped out from the back of Rudolf's throat. He scratched his muzzle and smiled. "I need to be more of a freak like you. Minus the tinsel. And you…" He hung a red ornament on the end of an antler and watched the flames flicker in its swaying reflection. "Maybe you can be more of a freak like me. I can keep my promise if you'll stay with me." A dim glow of appreciation. Jack watched the ornament swing. "But I do need something."

15 - BATTLE!

Krampus' house looked out of place in Hell. A traditional German cottage, with ornate woodwork and trim, fairy-tale-like shutters, and wood shingles, looked so terribly out of place. Quaint, cozy, warm and inviting. It just didn't belong. The flower boxes hanging outside the windows long held nothing but barren dirt, which the trolls dutifully cleared of cobwebs, for even weeds didn't grow in them. Long-dead trees flanked the house, such that if imagined just right, one could picture this home in some ancient forest. The flagstone path winded through the dead trees, and was swept clean by the trolls, who all seemed happy to serve their Krampus. And it wasn't just the path and the flowerboxes that needed tending, for in Hell, soot was a constant nemesis. Trolls washed the windows, swept the chimney, mopped the roof, and when the day finished, a new team would arrive to start the cleaning all over yet again.

And the cleaning didn't end at the front door, for soot made its way inside as well. So trolls dusted, wiped, scrubbed and swept endlessly inside. All happy to serve. Aside from trolls, and ceaseless soot, being in Hell, and well, having a Christmas demon for an owner, the cottage was otherwise homey and inviting. Deep red, nearly brown, mahogany maybe, floral patterns bloomed across the wall—painted, not printed, mind you, as was the custom in the old days. The couch and chairs and tables were all carved in the finest detail, including the cupboard which looked suspiciously like the cupboard in Crusty's cottage—a hand-carved winter scene of Krampus and Santa cheerily heading forth—together—some Christmas Eve long ago. But, instead of an ancient cap hanging off the side of this cupboard, an old photo hung, just slightly askew. An ancient photo, the colors had been painted in over the black and white print. But what photo might hold Krampus' attention seemed even odder—like some family portrait, thirteen men peered back. Some smiled, others pouted. Some were tall, and others quite short. Fat and skinny. Festive and frightening. Clearly related, brothers perhaps, though a few of them looked rather trollish.

Krampus sat in his favorite chair, looking outside at the rocky, barren view, sipping a dainty cup of tea, pinky-out. And when he heard a far-off cry, his eyes turned aside. He beamed a huge smile at the troll serving him tea. "They're here, troll," he said, just as a dark sinister cloud brooded about his face. His voice deepened and grew gravelly. "I'm going Christmas shopping."

That far off cry belonged to Jack, who charged along the narrow path on Rudolf. He screamed another war cry, waving about a meat tenderizer which looked like a club in his hands. A new tape sash carried brightly colored ball ornaments, bouncing as he galloped along. His Santa sack, tied around his neck, whipped about like a long cape.

And Krampus wasn't the only one to hear Jack's cry. Santa moved quickly, using a rock and a stick to pry out one of the hinge pins from the gate, stopping when he heard Jack. He closed his eyes and sighed, frustrated. "Rumpus," he grumbled, rushing back to work. "We must hurry. Candi, tell him I don't want any help-" But just as the pin finally fell, Krampus tackled Santa from the side—a dark blur whooshing past as he and Santa disappeared.

Candi pushed her face to the bars, eyes darting side to side. "Santa?" But Santa was gone. She looked down, way down below, to where trolls emerged from a cave and stomped up the path. "Snowballs," she gasped. Across the way, near a bridge of rocky pillars, Krampus let go of Santa, tumbling him into a pile of lost toys. Santa winced, arching his back, reaching under and pulling out the remnants of an old wooden train. His eyes widened, seeing Krampus bounding toward him for another tackle and he did the only thing he could think of. He beaned Krampus in the head with the train, admittedly not the most skillful defense, but desperate times, desperate measures.

And the lack of skill wasn't missed on Krampus, who stopped, stunned and rubbing where the train cracked against him. "Ow! Really?"

Santa hopped to his feet, and they began circling one another. Under normal circumstances, Santa might have a witty comeback, perhaps something about the crazy train finally reaching its destination. But Santa was tired and crabby and not in the mood for jokes. Plus, as often as he and Krampus had butted heads over the years, he had never seen Krampus so off-kilter. "This isn't us, Krampus!" He cautiously reached for a long, thick dead branch.

"And what do you know about *us*, Kringle?"

"We used to ride together."

"Before you stole Christmas!" Krampus lunged, charging at Santa, and just as he reached him, Santa jabbed the stick. Right into his belly. Krampus heaved as the wind knocked out of him, and his momentum launched him upward and over Santa, crashing down and rolling back to his feet. Krampus bared his teeth, flashing his long tongue with a howl. Santa shrieked and fled, hearing another one of Jack's war cries getting close.

But it wasn't a war cry that Santa had heard. As Rudolf charged around a sharp bend, his footing missed and they slid over the cliff's edge. And in a moment of panic, Jack forgot...Rudolf flies! The reindeer continued on his turn through the air, nose burning bright, and galloping back onto the path. They rushed down the last stretch toward the jail, leaping over toys, logs, and boulders, to round a corner into a hard stop. Jack flipped over Rudolf's antlers and landed a foot-kick to the troll's chest.

"Jackie!" Candi grinned.

The troll scrambled to his feet and rushed Jack, who shouted "Water bomb!" before ripping one of the ornaments from his sash and fast balling it at the troll. It shattered against the bewildered troll's head, drenching him with water. The troll shook its head as Jack observed, rather disappointed, "Well, that was kinda...lame." He lobbed a second ornament at the troll, shouting "Flour bomb!" Poof! The troll now coughed through white dust, wiping a pasty, sticky mess from its eyes, growling.

"How's that supposed to help?" Candi asked. "You're just making him angry."

"Distraction," Jack beamed, nodding back. "Rudolf!" Rudolf snorted, charging and scooping the troll with his antlers, racing away with the troll waving its arms and legs in protest, passing Krampus and Santa at the pillar bridge. Had Santa a moment to think, he might have thought to call over Rudolf to help him escape. But he didn't think. And he didn't call. And he was out of room to run with Krampus on his tail. He paused at the edge of a deep crevice; tiny rocks skittering underneath his feet into the dark below. He turned back to Krampus, down into the deep, and then leaped over to the first jagged rocky pillar. His leap fell short, however. He tossed his stick just in time to free his hands so that he could grip the pillar's edge, and he hung as the stick rolled across the surface, nearly twisting off the other side. Krampus reached the crevice and skidded to a halt, grinning and enjoying the sight of Santa hanging.

Santa glared over his shoulder, grunting and groaning has he climbed. "Steal Christmas?" Santa asked at last. "Ha!" He climbed a little more, his boot loosening rocks as he stretched and pushed, feeling less and less a little too-oldy as he had of late. "Steal from who? You?"

"It was ours," Krampus sniveled.

Santa pulled his knee up onto the pillar and climbed up, bent over and huffing as he caught his breath. Finally, he straightened, the thought of Krampus' complaint coming clear, and in his most you're-an-idiot tone he could muster (and sounding suspiciously like Jack) he semi-chuckled, semi feigned surprise, "No, it wasn't." Krampus groaned and leapt. Santa spun about, swiping up the stick and swinging like he was aiming for a home run. The branch whacked Krampus hard in the chest and split in two. Krampus flipped back, landing with a thud.

Back by the jail, Rudolf guarded the troll, who was bound and struggling at his feet. Jack used the hinge pin and meat tenderizer to tap out the second pin, and once it finally fell, Kevin kicked down the gate. Candi ran to Jack, wrapping herself around the surprised elf and kissing him. "Hope!" she beamed.

"Hope? What?"

Candi turned back to Kevin. "There's always hope."

Kevin scanned past the elves, nodding towards Santa and Krampus. "Tell that to Santa," he said. In the far distance, as Santa readied to leap to the next pillar, Krampus stomped his cloven hoof and a powerful blast radiated out. The pillar crumbled and shifted, tilting along with it. Santa rocked back and forth to keep his bearings, and then finally used the falling momentum to leap over to the next pillar, only to find Krampus already standing before him.

Jack started to hop onto Rudolf, but Candi yanked him back. "Santa. He said don't help him."

"But-" Jack started to protest, pushing forward.

Candi gripped his forearm, adamant. "Given the choice between Santa or the children, who do you think he'd want you to help?" Jack grunted, pacing and tangled in his conflicting thoughts. He couldn't just leave Santa here. He watched Krampus and Santa circling one another.

"Christmas is bigger than either one of us, Krampus," Santa said.

"You reward the Nice kids. I punish the Naughty ones. It's not any bigger than that."

Santa leapt to the other side of the crevice and turned back. "Oh, Krampus…"

"But you went and took all the glory. Stopped bringing me along. Replaced me for lumps of coal. What kind of punishment is that?" Krampus leapt, punching Santa and knocking him onto his back. A small band of flying reingoyles darted for Jack. Santa knew he had to keep Krampus occupied until the children were safe. He scrawled away backwards, grasping for any random lost toy he could find and pitching them at Krampus.

Jack and Candi urged the Naughty kids on and into the Santa-sack. One-by-one they climbed inside, shocked at the endless red interior. "All the way to the back," Candi shouted, trying to keep the opening clear…but there was no back! The sack seemed to go on forever and ever. As Jack nudged Randy Jones, he was in such a hurry that he didn't even give pause, thinking he might have recognized him from somewhere. When a reingoyle swooped down and then sprang up from the cliff's edge, surprising them, Jack reacted on instinct. He dropped his hold on the sack and swung at the beast with the meat tenderizer…knocking it out of the air and sending it tumbling down in a single blow. Jack gasped at what he had done, wide-eyed. "Don't." He watched the animal tumble down into the dark. "Oh! Don't tell Santa about that."

Kevin pointed to where Krampus knelt over Santa. "I don't think he'll care."

"Kevin, help Candi." Jack shoved his end of the sack opening to Kevin. "I've gotta-"

"Jackie, no!" Candi insisted. "Santa said no."

"Take Rudolf," he ordered, bounding away towards Santa, who scrounged around for a Magic 8 Ball.

"It was one thing to punish them with a switch and a rod," Santa snapped. "But then you started dragging them here!"

Krampus frowned. "They need to learn their lesson!"

"By stealing their voices? What you do isn't teaching." He still couldn't get his fingers around the 8 Ball. "It's torture. And I want no part in it. That's why we stopped riding together."

"So the Naughty List keeps growing."

"And now you're coming after my own with Rumpus and Candi? That crosses a new line."

"What do you care what Krampus does?"

Santa gave up on the Magic 8 Ball, threw a powerful punch to Krampus' face and rolled over so that he now knelt over Krampus. "Because I'm Santa Claus," he snapped. And in a determined and furious yet not-so-Santa-y moment, he added, "Dammit!"

Krampus gave a slight nod, as if letting Santa in on a tiny secret. "Not for much longer." He kicked up, launching Santa up and over his head and over the cliff.

Santa fell, tumbling through the air. "Oh…ho…ho…"

Candi's cry yanked Krampus' attention, just as Jack reached the first pillar, skidding to a halt and watching Santa tumble into the deep. "Santa!" he cried out, as a swarm of reingoyles and gargoyles rose up.

Krampus pointed towards the Naughty kids. "Hurry, trolls! Keep the children!" As he charged towards Jack, easily moving from one pillar to the next, Jack volleyed between him and Santa. And just as Krampus grabbed for Jack, Jack did the only thing that made sense to him. He jumped. Right over the cliff. "Fool!" Krampus shot, watching Jack fall a moment before bounding away towards Candi.

Jack tumbled past several gargoyles, even knocking some of them out of the air as he ricocheted between them. A surprised few turned and followed Jack, who managed to latch onto the twisted horn of a passing reingoyle. The beast spiraled downward as Jack climbed up onto his back, and when Jack got him to straighten out its flight, it protested—bucking and twisting and trying to shake Jack from his back like some demented bull at a rodeo. But Jack held on until it finally gave up control, and then he dove for Santa. He swooped down, much like he did when rescuing Feliz, riding alongside Santa, gripping Santa's arm and helping him onto the animal's back.

Santa. Was. Stunned. "Rumpus?" he gasped, getting his bearings before letting out a hearty ho-ho-ho.

"Hang tight!" Jack hair-pinned the beast and climbed as the gargoyles caught up.

"We've got company," Santa observed. Jack looked over his shoulder, ripped an ornament from his sash and handed it to Santa. "What's this?"

"Pepper bomb. I think."

Santa threw the ornament, shattering it against one of the gargoyles in a puff of pepper. It stalled and started sneezing uncontrollably as the second gargoyle rushed and latched onto Santa's back. The reingoyle they rode upon whipped about as Santa attempted to shake the gargoyle. They bounced about through the air in the most unglorious fashion (unless bullriding is your kind of thing), with Santa pressing down on Jack's head with one hand (to keep from falling) and reaching back for the gargoyle with the other. At last, and much to Jack's relief, Santa finally grabbed the little demon by the scruff of its neck, shook it furiously a few times for good measure, and threw it aside.

"Candi!" Jack called, diving towards the jail where Candi and Kevin urged the last of the Naughty kids into the sack.

Candi looked up, wincing at their approach with a reingoyle/gargoyle horde swarming above. She looked down, grimacing at the Krampus-horde thumping up from below. "Oh!" she nudged the last kid along a little too furious. "Hurry! Hurry! Hurry!" The boy stumbled and slid deep inside as Candi cinched the sack shut and thrust it into Kevin's hands. "Do. Not. Let. Go," she said, her eyes frowning for emphasis. She climbed onto Rudolf. "Hop on!" As soon as she yanked up Kevin, they shot away, joining Jack and Santa in a race back up to Kevin's fireplace.

Kevin looked back to where Krampus and the trolls raced up the path. "We got trouble!" he shouted, as a reingoyle head-butted Rudolf from behind. Rudolf tumbled, flinging Kevin through the air. Kevin shouted for help, scrambling for the sack of Naughty kids that slipped from his grip. Jack corkscrewed down to fetch the sack as gargoyles closed in on it. Jack charged into them, scattering them with blows from the meat tenderizer and catching the sack.

"Oh," Jack groaned, looking apologetically with the meat tenderizer, handing the sack to Santa.

"I think we can overlook that," Santa winked. "Given the circumstances."

Candi and Rudolf shook off their dizziness as Jack and Santa whizzed past them. "Can you make the jump?" he asked Santa.

"A few feet more." Santa carefully climbed onto the reingoyle's back, again pushing down on Jack's head for balance and support. He teetered as they approached, finally jumping over into Kevin's spot on Rudolf's back.

Candi gritted her teeth, looking over to Kevin tumbling about. "I told him to hold on."

"Jackie will get him!"

"Kevin," Jack called, gargoyles closing in. He tossed him the meat tenderizer, and Kevin fumbled, but finally made the catch. As he first swung, however, he began to fall. Jack rushed past him, crashing into the scattering gargoyles, and did his hairpin trick so that Kevin landed hard on the reingoyle's back.

"Ow!" Kevin groaned, hands going to his crotch, feeling as if he had just been kicked there with the force of a thousand kicks.

"Eee," Jack winced, feeling Kevin's pain. "Sorry about that."

They charged past Rudolf, to where Krampus was now perilously close to the fireplace. Santa handed the sack of Naughty kids to Kevin. "Get the children safe!"

"Yes, sir!" Jack shouted, racing away.

"And, Jackie!" Santa called. "Don't let that beast through!" The last of the reingoyles trailed after Jack. Santa turned to Candi. "We need to buy him a dash of time." Candi swooped around, veering down on Krampus and the trolls. Krampus swatted at them and missed as trolls scattered, some falling over the cliff.

Jack landed at the fireplace and hopped off, yanking the Santa sack from Kevin and swinging it at the last of the reingoyles on his tail. The Naughty kids inside grumbled with the blow that knocked the enemy out of the air. Jack pitched the sack through the flames and urged Kevin to step through the fire so he could get back to battling Krampus. He hit the reingoyle on the rump, sending him galloping away down the path and charging towards Krampus.

"You're coming with me, right?" Kevin pleaded.

"I have to help Candi."

"But Santa said-"

"Get the children safe and don't let the beast through."

"Please!?" Jack stopped, mid-step towards the battle. Compassion grabbed hold of him. His shoulders relaxed. This was the tough Goth-kid. The boss of everyone. Saying *please*. He must be scared, Jack thought. Or, he learned a lesson. Maybe both. He gently nudged Kevin through the flames.

"Ho! Ho! Ho!" Santa called as Rudolf dived again. Between the charging reingoyle and the dive-bombing Rudolf, with his nose burning bright and bowling over the trolls, the Krampus-horde scattered again. Jack laughed, hopping through behind Kevin. Furious, Krampus kicked a troll over the ledge and resumed his race towards the fireplace.

Rudolf looped, diving into the flames. Rudolf, Candi, and Santa charged through the fireplace in a puff of red and green light, tumbling across the living room floor. As Santa tumbled, he shot an ice-blue light from his palms towards the fireplace, so that the flames froze blue, and Krampus' face slammed into it from the other side.

"They won't learn!" Krampus growled, pounding against the frozen ice flames. "You take those kids and they'll be right back on the Naughty list next year. You'll see!"

Santa looked outside and back into the fireplace. "It's almost sun-up. Sure you want to continue this?" To which, Krampus yelled in frustration. "Maybe next year?" he jabbed.

Candi's jaw dropped. "Are you seriously antagonizing him?"

Santa shot her a look, but relented...Candi was right. "Hey, Krampus?" Krampus paused. "Crusty says hey." And then the strangest thing happened. As Krampus thought, his demeanor changed. His rage subsided and he cocked his head askew. He smiled and bowed, much to the surprise of Jack, Candi and Santa. "Um...he also said something about biscuits and tea?"

"Krampus," Krampus paused. "Would like that. And, Kringle? 'Til next Christmas." His sinister laugh crescendoed and then faded as the ice flames melted into nothing.

Santa rolled over to his feet. "Hoo, wee! Haven't felt this alive in...years. Though don't tell The Missus. She'll think I'm looking for trouble. Crusty?!" he called. "A little help? Again?" The white wisps swirled in, as Santa spoke at the ceiling. "I told him you said hey. Probably should have opened with that." A much older-sounding Ho-ho-ho chimed from the space about them, and Santa, appreciating the sound, let out his own hearty Ho-ho-ho. Aside from a sack full of Naughty kids, Christmas would be okay.

16 - SANTA'S SECRET

Had the Goth-kids woken up and looked outside, they would have seen the most peculiar sight…but they didn't wake up. Crusty had taken good care of them and made sure they were resting well after their blows with Krampus. Outside in their cul-de-sac were two teams of reindeer, two sleds, a couple elves, Santa, and a much more humbled version of their very own Kevin. It was just before dawn, and the crisp air filled with countless stars like an abundance of Christmas wishes— twinkling, expectant, full of hope and dream.

As a Naughty-kid stepped from Jack's Santa-sack and climbed into a second sack, Santa surveyed the sky, looking East and habitually checking for the time on a watch he wasn't wearing. "Okay, let's get these children home before sun-up. Jack, you're with me. Candi, you take the other team."

Kevin tugged at his sleeve. "Can I help?"

"Sorry, son," Santa nodded, just as Candi tugged at his other sleeve, urging him down to speak in a hush.

"It will do him good to help," she insisted.

"But then we'd have to circle back."

And then Candi's big eyes grew even bigger, all doe-eyed. "Please?"

Santa sighed, only slightly annoyed, feeling hurried. "Fine."

"And, Santa? Can I please take your team instead?"

And then…The Santa Look. He put so much effort into that frown. "Nobody rides Santa's team except Santa! How hard is that to understand?" And when she flashed her doe-eyes again, he snapped, "No. Don't make your eyes all bubbly like that." But for a moment he reflected on the night he had, and her part in it all, and he relented again, but only a little. "But maybe…maybe I can make an exception and let Rudolf lead your team." Candi's appreciative smiles slipped out a giggle, just as Santa threw a playful glare at her. "Seeing as how you've been taking him out for joyrides."

Her face twisted up…busted, and she quickly turned away to Jack. "Am I going to see you later?" she asked, and this seemed to be the oddest question to Jack. "You've met Krampus, so the whole perma-swear thing…"

"Oh!" Jack shook away his confusion. "I do not want to live with Krampus. Definitely."

"But that doesn't mean you want to come home."

As Candi was perhaps the only one at The Pole who could understand him, Jack grew sad. Why was it so hard for her to understand? "I don't belong at The Pole, Candi." And now Santa grew sad, too…his grumpiness returning, so much so that Jack and Santa's ride together remained silent, with Jack constantly dodging his side-glances.

"Now, you're all grumpy-face again," Jack said at last.

"Randy Jones," Santa nodded. Jack hopped to his feet and called into the sack for Randy, helping him climb out a moment later. While waiting for the sleigh to come up over his house, Randy witnessed the exchange between Jack and Santa, which made him uncomfortable. Christmas songs and stories were nothing but jolly; certainly not full of Santa bickering with elves. "I could have gotten them all out, quietly," Santa grumbled. "If you would just do what you're told."

"I didn't *ask* you to go and rescue Candi," Jack snapped. "What I asked for was for you to just open the door to Krampus!"

"Don't! Just don't!" Santa glared. Randy's eyes widened as he looked away, to the blur of houses scrolling below. "I didn't want your help!"

"But you needed by help!"

"Only because you helped me in the first place!"

Jack stood on the seat, defiant as ever. "Only because, *once again*, you didn't give me what I wished for!"

Santa mocked him through gritted teeth. "Well, maybe we're too much alike in that we don't care what other people want!"

"But-" Jack thought, starting to chuckle. "You're Santa." And then Santa got to thinking the absurdity of their arguing, and he chuckled too. Jack sat down again. "Being nice is so freakin' hard."

"No, Jackie," Santa sighed. "Being nice isn't hard. Doesn't make it easy just the same. Just be mindful."

"It was all my fault."

"And yet, it wasn't all your fault. Yes, all these Christmases your wish has been to meet Krampus, but there was more to it, wasn't there? Something I just couldn't give you."

Jack thought. "To run away from The Pole?"

"Nobody is a prisoner at the North Pole. If you want to go, then go, but I can't give that to you. That's something you need to take."

"I don't belong there."

"The North Pole is your home, Jackie. Of course you belong there." Santa paused on his words, biting his lower lip. "More than you can fathom." Randy grimaced…okay. Santa nodded back to him, telling Jack it was time.

"Randy Jones." Jack said. He thought back to his first house. "Randy Jones!" And then further back to the night at the post office. "Ah! Randy Jones!" Santa and Randy Jones didn't know what to make of Jack, who put up a finger and instructed Santa with a "Wait up!" He looked into his sack and reached about, shooing Naughty kids out of the way. "Where is it? Where is it?"

Guessing what Jack was thinking, Santa whispered so no one else could hear, "Kommensiefür Randy Jones." And with that, a toy whizzed through the sack and smacked into Jack's palm.

"Gah!" Jack winced at the sting, pulling out the Decimator.

Santa looked over through a side-glance. Randy's eyes grew wide. "Decimator!" he shrieked, snatching it from Jack's hands and hugging it tight. Jack's delight only gave way when he saw Santa's subtle disapproval…and when Randy's eyes grew sad, realizing. "But," he said, "I'm on the Naughty List." He held the toy at arm's length, fighting to keep it, urging himself to give it back to Jack. Jack looked to Santa with pleading eyes…can I give it to him? Santa sighed, rolled his eyes and nodded…whatever.

"You can keep it."

Wide-eyed, Randy darted between the two…really? But he couldn't keep it. That was part of his lesson. He pushed it back to Jack. "Maybe next year."

Jack took the toy back, disappointed. "Okay, then." He grabbed Randy by the shoulders and held him over the side of the sleigh.

Of course, Randy protested. "Wait-what?!" He kicked and squirmed and tried to reach out for the safety of the sleigh. "Santa!"

And Santa's response was also not the hearty Ho-ho-ho of Christmaslore. Instead, Randy got a half-hearted "Be nice, kid. Ho-ho-ho."

Jack dropped him over his house as Randy's shouts of terror gave way to hooting. Sherbert-colored sparks flew out and ignited a twisting-turning water-slide-like path downward. Enshrouded in the sparkling light, Randy laughed, zipping down towards his house. He passed through the roof as if he were a falling angel, slipping through walls, studs, wires, pipes, and finally flashing through red and green sparks through the STAR WARS poster on his bedroom wall. He slid through and into bed, already asleep. But moments later, he awoke, looking at his wall as if remembering. He rolled over and knelt before the poster, feeling it as if expecting it to be something other than a poster. Perfectly normal. "What a weird dream," he thought, before realizing…It's Christmas!

The sherbert-colored beams shot out from Santa and Candi's sleighs as more children slid home. Kevin watched the world blur by. "How do you see anything?" Candi peered over the edge…the world looked perfectly normal to her. She shrugged his thought away just as she tried to shrug away her sadness. "Hope," Kevin reminded her. "Right?"

She smiled a sad smile at him, thoughtful, but nodded in agreement. "Hope."

From a distance, it looked as though sherbert-colored swirling beams shot out from the sleighs rapid-fire at the houses below. But Polar Magic moved time normally inside the sleighs.

"When I saw you were getting ready to run away," Santa began. "I knew this had to be the year you finally met Krampus."

"You knew?"

"I expected you'd jump all over the *Ride With Santa* contest, but when you didn't bite I honestly thought your plan was to steal Rudolf. I really didn't want you running into Krampus on your own."

"So you cancelled Christmas," Jack said, flatly.

"The Missus gave me an idea. If I cancelled it, I could better see what steps you'd take. Like stealing the Naughty List."

"I didn't actually steal it," Jack began, but stopped on The Santa Look. He sighed, as busted as Candi.

"And then you—or Candi—got Christmas uncancelled. I threw caution to the wind and made a plan that would only work if you thought it was your plan working against me."

Jack shook his head. Embarrassed. Ashamed. Why couldn't he just do the right thing? "I'm sorry."

"It's okay. All part of the plan."

"To meet Krampus?"

"Oh!" Santa beamed, the rosiness of his cheeks burning brighter than Jack had seen in a long time. "So much bigger than that, Jackie!" He nodded, "Amy Doohan."

Jack looked inside the sack. The last of their Naughty kids. He helped her climb out, and she gave Santa the biggest hug. "Thank you," she said, sincere.

"Thank Jackie," Santa nodded. She wrapped her arms about Jack for the biggest bear hug, like he was one of her stuffed toys. Initially taken aback, Jack returned the hug, with intense joy and love overwhelming him. Santa smiled, appreciating the moment, knowing that Jack was the right choice.

Jack wiped away a stray tear, leading Amy to the edge of the sleigh. "Be good, kid."

As Candi re-approached the cul-de-sac where Kevin's house was, Kevin smiled. "This has been fun," he said.

"You've got a weird sense of fun, kid. There's your house."

"I'm going to forget all this, aren't I?"

"I hope not." Kevin climbed onto the edge of the sleigh, wind tousling his long black hair. "Be nice, Kevin."

He teetered on his balance, but turned back a devilish grin. "No promises. But I'll try."

"Well, if you can't be nice, then make like an elf."

He hopped off with a laugh. Candi smiled, rushing to the edge to watch his descent, and for a moment she considered the rules...Naughty or Nice? Naughty or Nice? And, like Jack, she knew the difference between the two, and yet somehow they at times were the same thing. She tossed something into the sherbert light that wound its way into Kevin's bedroom. In a flash of red and green, Kevin slipped through the wall and into bed, asleep. And, like Randy, and much of the other Naughty kids, he woke up, looking about with the strangest sensation of having forgot something. *It's Christmas!* he thought, nothing more special than that, as special as that was. He felt something under the covers. He reached under the blanket and pulled out the oddest surprise...a meat tenderizer. But how did that get there, he wondered. Was he sleep walking? He thought some more, curious. And more thinking as random thoughts and images of his adventure popped in and out of focus in his mind, and then...a huge smile. It really was Christmas!

Indeed it was, or very nearly it was, for the Chicago suburbs anyway. Up in the sky, Jack flashed one last sleep-ball. It shot up, glowing, sparkly-wet. And as the sun peeked over the horizon, the snowball melted into a wet nothing.

"I'm going to miss that," he said. "As lame as it is."

Santa and Candi's sleighs met and then headed up high into the sky, back towards The Pole.

"I wasn't always Santa, you know."

Jack considered that with a twisted face. He always knew Santa's name was Kringle, but he never imagined Kringle as anything but Santa. "Guess I never really thought on it."

"When I was chosen, I was an elf not much unlike you. *Fly for Santa* was the perfect opportunity to see who might just become the next Santa." His eyes arched, a touch of his old tiredness returning. "I'm about ready to pass on the reins."

Wide-eyed, Jack reached for the leather straps. "Really?!"

Santa nudged him away. "No! Not now!"

"Oh."

"But soon. Becoming Santa brings changes. You get tall. Age differently."

"And you get fat?" Jack smiled.

"Yes," Santa mocked. "You get fat. Though I reckon that has more to do with cookies. Crusty chose me-"

"Crusty?!" Of course, Crusty! Jack thought. No wonder he was so ancient. No wonder he was so tall. He must have been Santa before Santa was…Santa. Oh, he felt overwhelmed. Mind. Blown. Overwhelmed.

"He chose me," Santa paused, hesitant, seriously making sure, and sure he was right. "Much for the same reason I'd like to choose…you." Jack blinked, silent. Santa nodded with a look to ensure that Jack got the point. "I've been Santa for so long, nobody remembers Crusty was the one before me. Except The Missus, of course. You're a natural born leader, Jackie."

"Leader?" Jack harrumphed. "No. Everyone hates me."

"And yet they follow you. Who else could have inspired a factory uprising to get Christmas uncancelled?" Jack thought…maybe Candi? "And who else can I choose? Feliz? He's a bully. Plus, I need someone who can handle Krampus. Feliz just wet himself."

"No way!" Jack laughed.

Santa laughed with him, but then grew serious. "Share that with nobody."

Jack held up a Scout's Honor salute. "Just me and Emily Dickinson."

Santa chuckled. "And nobody flies quite like you do, Jackie. Elves. They're followers. And you, and Candi, are definitely not followers. You have big hearts. You care about others, even if you go through life pretending to hate everyone and everything."

161

"I don't hate everyone," Jack lamented. "But I'm not so sure I can be a leader when everyone hates me."

"Well, you coming home, or should I drop you off somewhere cold, like Chicago?"

Jack thought, watching Candi fly ahead. "I don't like cold."

17 - MANY REASONS

As Candi descended around Gumdrop Mountain over The Pole, she could see and hear the end-of-the-year celebrations continuing down below. Cheers erupted as soon as someone pointed out the light from Rudolf's nose, and everyone scampered towards Headquarters. She landed her reindeer team and was met by some stable hands who congratulated and applauded her, which made no sense to her at all. She gave Rudolf a hug and a kiss, and patted him on his side, thanking him for their greatest adventure yet. A dim glow of appreciation returned as the stable hands led the team into the barn for food, water, and much-needed rest.

Candi stood alone in the cold plain. The wind blew her blond hair and howled a loneliness. She looked up to the empty sky and sighed…well, that's that. She headed back to Headquarters, and as she stepped through the sliding glass doors, she was met with the most wild applause. She stood motionless, bewildered at the excitement among the throng of elves. The Missus handed her a peppermint ale as Crusty hugged her. "Merry Christmas, Candi Kane," he greeted.

"Merry Christmas," she returned, but there was no merry in her greeting. Her misplaced faith in the perma-swear failed. Krampus was indeed real! And Jackie was gone.

The Missus looked past Candi to the cold outside. "Where's-"

"They were right behind me," Candi shrugged, sipping her ale. "Until they weren't." She gulped the rest of her drink as The Missus rubbed her shoulders.

"Someone get this girl another peppermint ale! She's earned it. Going up against the likes of Krampus? Saving the children?"

Crusty squealed with delight. "Did you see the way Jack caught Santa?"

Now, Candi was even more bewildered. "How did you see-"

"You two are heroes!" exclaimed The Missus.

"I don't feel like a hero."

Crusty smiled. "A quality among true heroes."

Santa barged through the doors and another wave of excited cheers rolled through Headquarters. "Ho! Ho! Ho! Merry Christmas!"

"Welcome home, Kringle," said The Missus, greeting him with a hug and kiss. Candi saw him alone, feeling defeated.

"Kringle!" Crusty looked about. "But, where's Jackie?"

Santa smiled to Candi with a wink. "Someone tripped over a saddle in the reindeer barn."

The doors opened, and Jack stumbled in sneezing uncontrollably. "Stupid saddle!" More sneezes. "Stupid pepper bombs!"

"Pepper bombs went off," Santa said, beaming.

Candi was all smiles, as Jack was all sneezes. "Snowballs!" he sneezed. "Stupid-" Another sneeze. Jack saw the crowd and then stifled yet another sneeze, acting cool. "I mean, whatever." He nearly jumped back outside as they all cheered for him. Candi rushed him for a hug.

"Jackie! You're home!"

He was taken aback by the hug. Taken aback by the cheers. By the crowd...looking at him. By how the weight of their looks felt so heavy and yet so light at the same time, as if something had changed in them, and maybe something had changed in himself. They were looking at him, and they saw *him*. Past the eyeliner, and past the pale makeup, past the Goth clothes and into his heart. They saw him. Just *Jack*. And this was the complete opposite of everything he always said he wanted, and yet he knew, this was exactly what he always really wanted. He dug deep into his pocket and presented Candi with her jack-o-lantern bat necklace. The one made festive with a Santa hat. "I wanted to give this to you. Again."

Candi took the necklace and held it close. She wanted to smile. She wanted to cry. She looked to Santa with heart-happy gratitude...she got her one Christmas wish.

Crusty patted Jack on the shoulder. "Welcome home, Santa."

The greeting surprised Jack and confused Candi. Jack looked up to Santa…huh?

Santa nodded. "If you choose to be."

Crusty clapped, and the crowd clapped with him. The applause grew, as did the cheers, such that several days later, Jack could still hear it ringing in his ears. He felt home. Finally, like he belonged at The Pole.

Overlooking the toy factory, Jack stood on the catwalk with Candi, Santa and The Missus. He tore off a sheet from the *Days To Christmas Eve* calendar and shouted out. "Okay, gang! Only three hundred and fifty days 'til next Christmas Eve!" He turned sly towards Santa. "Let's have some fun!" He cranked up the holiday music—which was festive, but with an angsty Goth-band twist. And he danced, not caring that the entire factory floor of elves watched him dance. Candi joined in the dancing as Santa and The Missus laughed in appreciation.

Through the ranks of the elves on the factory floor, some were dressed with hints of Jack's style—jet black hair there, dark eye-liner there, a few piercings scattered about. But none was more imitating than Feliz—who wore the dark eyeliner, and had the fake piercings, and had dramatically etched along the back of his work vest *RUMPUS*.

Feliz rolled his eyes, watching his new-found hero dance above them. "Whatta freak!"

The End.